Clementine's
Winter

SANDRA GOLDBACHER

A *Girl* *for all* *Time*®
BOOK

Typeset: thepixelpusher.co.uk

Although based on historical facts, the main characters are works of fiction.

First published in Great Britain in 2015
by Daughters of History Ltd.
Reg. No. 7057626
207 Regent Street, 3rd Floor
London W1B 3HH
United Kingdom

www.AGirlForAllTime.com

For Rodolpho & Ernie

Chapter 1

Ronnie had looked pinched and green for most of the journey from London, and just as the train slowed to pull into Oxbury station, he vomited noisily into the paper bag that had held the meat-paste sandwiches. Clementine sighed. They'd look even more of a mess now. She spat on her hankie to wipe his face and furrowed a comb through Ernie's sticky hair, straightening the labels round both the boys' necks and unknotting the straps of their gas masks.

"We've got to look smart or they'll split us up," she said, for the hundredth time, "And sweet and smiley, like nice, normal children."

"Fat chance of that," sniffed Ernie, as Clementine tugged her brothers and their cardboard suitcases down onto the platform. They joined the swarm of other labeled children as a sturdy woman with a clipboard bore down on them.

"Goodness, what a vast throng of you," the woman announced. "I'm Constance Pumphrey and I'm going to be finding you all new homes. Well, come along then!"

She herded the crocodile of reluctant children out of the station and down a muddy lane towards the village.

Everything smelt of poo and countryside and dirtied their school-shoes. There were even some cows in a field, which Clementine had only seen in books.

Trestle tables had been set up in the village square and country adults waited in suspicious groups, eyeing the London evacuees, as they filed in.

The children stood in little, anxious knots and the adults circled round, inspecting them. Some had been snapped up already, Clementine noticed. A pretty, gold-ringletted blonde girl, who looked like Shirley Temple in the films, was being ticked off the Pumphrey woman's clipboard and led away by a kind-looking couple.

A farmery looking man was feeling the calf muscles of a strong-looking older boy. He grinned over at Clementine and raised his eyebrows.

"Like a Roman slave market, isn't it?" he called.

The Pumphrey woman tutted if people did too much inspecting, "This isn't Selfridges' Bargain Basement, you know! All the children have to find families!" But it didn't actually stop them eyeing the children up like cattle for sale.

Clementine could barely breathe. She didn't know if she should want to be inspected or to be ignored. Maybe if nobody chose them they'd be put back onto the London train. They could be walking back up Camden High Street, and tucked up in bed with cocoa by midnight, listening to the baby snuffling and dad coming back in, grumpy from his warden duty. Or she could be singing down the Underground shelter in Camden Town, if a raid was on.

It was quite fun down there and people really liked hearing her sing. Madame Pearl said any sort of performance in front of an audience was good practice for an artiste.

Anyway, she'd rather be bombed in London, with their house caught on fire, than put up with this humiliation. It was far worse than an audition. They weren't cows and pigs!

A fish-faced woman sidled over and started examining her scalp. "I'll take the girl if she doesn't have lice," she announced. She had a funny drawly country accent.

"She did once," piped up Ernie, "But don't worry, we brought the nit comb wiv us." The fish-faced woman scuttled quickly away.

"Ern! Shut up!" Clementine snarled, mortified.

The sky was beginning to darken and more and more of the children were pairing up with new families. Clementine was cold in her best, pink coat that Gran had made for her, and the boys were shivering.

Amongst the tense knots of people, the only smiling faces seemed to belong to a gang of girls in blue uniforms, threading their way purposefully through the square. A shiny-faced girl handed Clementine a mug of sweet tea.

"It's much harder if you want to all stay together," she whispered. "People think boys are more trouble. Unless they're strong and old enough to work."

4

"Nobody's splitting us up," Clementine clutched Ronnie and Ernie to her. The girl smiled kindly and gave Ronnie a Rich Tea biscuit.

Rain was starting to fall. They were the last children left in the chilly, darkening square. The Pumphrey woman sighed,

"Well if you will insist on being so stubborn..." And she marched them over to her car.

They drove in silence through the village, shut-up and dead looking in the blackout. Clementine pressed her face up against the window, gazing into the darkness of the unknowable, alien countryside. No Woolworths, no cinema, no playground, no Tube, no nothing.

She squeezed the boys' hands as they bumped onto a gravel driveway that led up to a tall, stone manor house. Carved into the gatepost were the words, 'Darkevaine House.' Ronnie's shoulders heaved again and Clementine just managed to put her hankie under his chin to catch the sicked-up Rich Tea biscuit.

Clementine was trying not to cry.

The children stood on the doorstep, drenched and rat-like, the black ink on the luggage labels round their necks running like tears. Mrs. Pumphrey tugged impatiently at the bell-pull. She'd had enough of doing good works now and wanted to be at home with her feet up and a gin and tonic in her hand.

A wary, pinched-faced woman answered the door, drying her hands on an apron.

"Mrs. Milvaine put her name down for an evacuee. This is she," said Mrs. Pumphrey as she pushed Clementine over the threshold.

"And these two come with her," she added quickly. "She was supposed to have come to the sorting party and choose but she didn't, so I chose for her. I do hope that's acceptable."

She pushed the boys inside, whispering to them, "Be polite to Mrs. Milvaine, now. She's going to be your new Auntie. Isn't that nice!" and retreated hastily through the rain back to her car.

Chapter 2

They stood, dripping dankly onto the rug, in the large, gloomy hallway. A grandfather clock chimed seven. The entrance was cluttered with boots and smelled of wet animal. Two dogs loped in and one snarled lazily at them. Ronnie clung to Clementine's soggy pink coat.

"Stand on the mat! You're soaking the rug," the thin woman snapped and walked quickly up the stairs with a martyred sigh. Stuffed stag heads stared down from the walls at them, their glass eyes glinting sadly through the gloom. A hasty, muttered conversation filtered down from upstairs as another dog wandered in and started sniffing the boys' groins. Ronnie began to whimper. He really hated dogs.

"He's just being friendly," said Clementine unconvincingly. She didn't like dogs much better herself and she began to writhe in embarrassment as the animal started to sniff at her, too. But Ernie bent down to pat him, pleased to be shown any sort of welcome in this wretched place.

A patch of light glowed at the top of the stairs and into it stepped a tall, pale figure wrapped in a trailing floral dressing gown, its feet encased in wellington boots. She was cradling something in her arms. Was it a baby? It writhed and its green eyes glowed. It was a very large black cat.

"Shush, Merlin. Oh dear they are very wet, aren't they?

I suppose we can't turn them out tonight. Well, as long as they like animals...," the woman said despondently.

"Do you?" She called down the stairs vaguely, "...like animals?"

"Answer Mrs. Milvaine," said Pinchy Face.

"We haven't met many," Clementine replied, trying to project her voice confidently up the stairs. And then dropped a curtsey suddenly, as she'd been trained to do at Madame Pearl's Stage School.

"Our Uncle Nando had a racing pigeon and it pooed on me head and I didn't mind," piped up Ernie.

"We love cats and dogs, of course," said Clementine shoving Ernie in the ribs. "Who doesn't!"

"Well I don't! You know I got bit by next door's Nipper," said Ronnie.

"Shush," Clementine put her hand over Ronnie's mouth.

Cynthia Milvaine smiled distractedly. "Well good...that's alright then. I far prefer animals to people."

She seemed both bored and exhausted by the conversation and turned away, nuzzling her face against Merlin.

"Put them all in Yellow Whiskers for tonight, Smithers."

"Thanks ever so much..." started Clementine, but Mrs.

Milvaine had already trailed away, cradling Merlin, and shut the door.

They trudged up three flights of stairs after Miss Smithers, trying not to bump their suitcases, which felt as though they were full of rocks, after their exhausting day and nothing proper to eat since the meat paste sandwiches.

Clementine would have given a week's rations for another cup of sweet tea and a biscuit from one of the smiling girls in blue. Maybe a Bourbon or a Custard Cream. Mustn't think of mum's cheese on toast with a face of brown sauce on the top. 'Put a stage-school smile on. Think of it as a part in a play,' she told herself, as they reached the top of the stairs – 'I'm the plucky evacuee: brave and funny, like Valerie Hobson in The Spy in Black.'

******

Yellow Whiskers, which was going to be their bedroom, didn't seem to be yellow in any way. The paneled walls were covered in paintings of dogs, cats and horses: 'Jason 1921', 'King 1930', 'Rex 1938'.

Clementine peeled the boys' soaking clothes off, rubbed them dry with a scratchy blanket and got them into their pyjamas. They smelled of mum's laundry. She buried her face in their collars to snuff it up, until the boys twisted away. Mum had hidden a toffee in the toes of each of their slippers and the sweet, melting taste made her feel even sadder. Mum, who worked so much that she didn't have time to think. Poor dad, who felt guilty about his bad eyes and not being able to fight and then got grumpy with everyone at home because of it. What were they doing now? She pushed the thought away. Were bombs falling?

When they were all three huddled in the high, creaky four-poster bed together, Clementine felt a wave of utter exhaustion ride her. Her legs were stiff and ached more than after three hours of ballet practice with Madame Pearl. Her head throbbed.

"Well, at least they didn't split us up," she said to the boys. Lightning flashed through the window, briefly lighting up the faces of 'Rex' and 'King' and 'Jason' and they all shrieked.

"Shall I sing you to sleep?" Clementine whispered gently.

"Oh gawd no…please don't!" said Ernie and they all laughed for the first time since they'd left Camden Town.

Chapter 3

Clementine slept fitfully and lumpily until dawn seeped around
the edges of the curtains. She woke in a pool of pleasingly
warm, then very unpleasantly cold, dampness. Ronnie had
wet the bed.

Clementine was tiptoeing down the hallway, with the soaked
bed sheet bundled underneath her nightie, when a door opened
on the landing and Miss Smithers' stretched shape loomed up.

"What do you have under there?" she said coldly, as though she
thought Clementine might be stealing something. What was
there to steal anyway - a flippin' deer head?

Clementine, mortified, pulled out the stinking sheet, like a
disemboweling.

"I'm ever so sorry…it's my little brother, he's upset. First night
away from home…He never usually…I was going to rinse it."
She felt her pale, freckled skin flush scarlet.

Miss Smithers held out her hands for the sheet, not unkindly,
almost as though it made her remember something fondly.
But her voice registered nothing.

"Mrs. Milvaine doesn't rise till midday. There's breakfast
waiting for you downstairs. Bring me down your ration books
please."

At least there was a proper inside toilet. Not like the outside lav
at home, with the squares of newspaper to wipe with. Mind you,

it was almost as freezing cold here. The bath was enormous and had clawed feet. They certainly weren't going to get into that.

Clementine tugged the boys into their clothes, piling almost all their woollies on in layers for warmth. For one daft moment she thought of putting on her red tap shoes for courage.

******

The children were starving by the time they'd found their way to the dining room. They huddled together at the end of a very long table. There were photographs of a young man in a soldier's uniform on a sideboard. And there he was, younger, in a school picture, with other boys wearing knickerbockers, in a crumbly courtyard and again holding a cricket bat. Clementine's eyes kept returning to them.

There was a dish covered with a silver salver like the toff family had in the Beano. Ernie raised it, like a magician, hoping to conjure up bacon and sausages, but revealed, instead, a small portion of corned beef and some powdered scrambled egg to go with the dry toast in the elaborate toast rack. But at least there was hot tea in a silver teapot.

"Blimey it's posh, isn't it?" said Ernie whistling. Clementine shushed him. "It's like Lord Snooty's house."

Miss Smithers appeared at the door and they jumped. Clementine got up to hand her their ration books.

"That Pumphrey busybody telephoned to me this morning. You're to go to the new evacuee school. Go back to the village

square and look for The Maypole. You'll see it. There's a
bicycle in the stables. You can share that."

It was drizzling as the children made their way through the
overgrown front garden and along the gravel drive, towards
an archway that led to what they thought must be the stables.
Though they'd never seen a stable, of course. It reminded
Clementine of The Secret Garden and Jane Eyre, which made
her feel a bit better about their adventure, and she walked
slightly on tiptoe with her chin tilted upwards, as she thought a
young heroine in a book would do.

The Snarler and the Groin Sniffer from last night lollopped over
to them and loped along, companionably, now they were fellow
inmates. They were joined by a small, shaggier friend who
jumped up and down and yapped.

******

Ernie pushed open the stable door, whistling, and then shrieked.

"Flipping, dundering hell," he swore, jumping backwards
against the others, as a shattering whinny ripped the air and a
massive jet-black beast rose, heft-hoofed.

A boy of about thirteen emerged from a stall. He was white with
anger.

"You don't bang into a stable like that! Are you mad?" He
worked to calm the anxious, brutal-seeming horse. It was the
largest animal the children had ever seen. "Shush Hercules…
shush there boy…"

13

They were all quivering. The boy had sand-coloured hair, which fell over his eyes.

"We didn't know that thing was gonna be in here," said Ernie.

"What did you expect to find in a stables, you clot!" said the cross boy. "It's called a horse!"

Clementine pulled herself up and put on her best stage voice to cover her embarrassment.

"Well, we were told to look for a bicycle, actually, by Mrs. Milvaine, with whom we are staying. And I don't appreciate you calling my brother a clot. We're from London."

The boy laughed. "Oh - well, that explains it then...actually."

Clementine sniffed. She did not like being made fun of. She spotted a bicycle wheel, under a pile of straw and started pulling at it. Its spokes were stuck under some tackle and she started getting redder and crosser. There was manure on the straw and it stuck to her hands.

"I hate the flipping country. Everything stinks!"

The boy strode over and shook the old bicycle free of the tack and straw. He put the handlebars into her hands, grinning. It was a rusty, heavy old thing and far too big for Clementine. She clambered onto it and pedaled judderingly onto the gravel drive. Ronnie and Ernie started running after her, followed by the three dogs.

"You're welcome, Miss London. No need to thank me," the boy called after her. "My name's Clinton, by the way, and it was nice to meet you too, Ginger!"

Rain plastered Clementine's hair over her eyes. Ginger! She was not ginger. Her hair was auburn like Anne of Green Gables and Rita Hayworth. How dare he! She fought to control the steering on the heavy handlebars, swerved into a stone urn and toppled off into a flower-bed, which was all mud and no flowers.

Clementine wanted to sink into the wet earth and disintegrate. She didn't want to paint on a brave face, pull up her socks, dig for victory, make do and mend or any of the other sick-making things the war was meant to make her pretend to be or do. She didn't want to rally her brothers and be in charge of their puking and peeing and whining and fear. Or suck up to mad old women who pretended cats were babies. She was only twelve and she wasn't one of those do-gooding Girl Guides who were so flippin' sensible and confident. She wanted to be in her red tap shoes practicing a routine from Forty Second Street.

Chapter 4

Ernie had been worried that they might be made to prance around a pole holding ribbons, but The Maypole turned out to be the village pub. The school had been moved there to fit in the London evacuees. Mrs. Pumphrey was there again, shooing the new children in. There were just two big classes - the 'Babies' Room' for the five to seven year olds, which was in the Saloon Bar and the 'Big Room' for the eight to fourteen year olds, which was in the Public Bar.

So Ronnie was in with the 'Babies' to his horror. Clementine and Ernie were squeezed onto a bench behind a shared school desk, which looked strange amongst the sticky pub furniture.

In the maroon velveteen gloom of the pub, the other children's faces were mysterious pale ovals. The smell of fuggy old beer and smoky dampness was faintly comforting and reminded Clementine of her dad and Granddad George. She could tell which children were Londoners like them – the pale, anxious, pinched-faced kids, trying to look cocky.

There were quite a few scabby-kneed shivery boys, puffing themselves up and swinging their skinny legs, but not as many girls. The girls who were there were mostly the friendly, village, shiny-faced, girls in blue uniforms. They all seemed nice, but what were they so happy about?

She spotted the golden hair of the posh Shirley Temple evacuee from the cattle market yesterday. She turned her shimmering head, smug with satin ribbons. Clementine ventured a smile, but when she saw Clementine and Ernie dripping mud, she wrinkled her tiny nose in an exaggerated way and turned away.

"Stuck up cow," muttered Ernie.

Clementine doodled her name on her exercise book, practising her signature for signing autographs one day. Her half-exercise book that is – the books had all been cut in half, like the pencils, to make them go further. All the ink pens and inkwells, sunk into the desks, were shared one between three.

The teacher came in: a glum-looking, stoopy man who said he was called Mr. Mildew. Could he really be called that, Clementine wondered. A few of the London children sniggered.

He seemed exhausted as he began a talk on, 'The War Effort on the Home Front.' Ernie dropped his pencil under the desk and started to edge forward with a little smile on his face.

Clementine became aware of a girl she hadn't noticed before. She was sitting in the darkest corner, at a pub table on her own, reading a book, which was propped behind her half exercise book. She was very unusual looking – with shiny dark hair, wide, violet eyes and long white fingers. She looked clever and her clothes were beautifully made, though simple and foreign-looking. Her shoes were shiny, like a butterscotch lozenge.

At that moment a shriek erupted from the desk in front.

The Shirley Temple girl ran her hands through her hair and screamed. One of her fat golden ringlets had been doused in black ink and, as she shook it, it splattered her ribbons and her pink blouse. Ernie snorted and popped up again at Clementine's desk. The dark haired girl locked eyes with Clementine and smiled.

But Ernie was for it. Mr. Mildew sighed wearily. "Come up to the front, child." Ernie puffed out his chest.

"Name?"

"Earnest Harper, sir."

"What possessed you to put Goldilocks' hair into the inkwell? If you give me a good enough answer I'll not give you six of the best with the slipper. So make it good."

Ernie shifted from foot to foot. "Well…it was just so tempting, hangin' there like a big sausage…"

The children sniggered and one or two gasped, everyone enjoying the drama. "And she looked really hoity-toity like at my sister Clem when we came in, just cos she's muddy and she's got horse poo on her sleeves."

The children roared with laughter and Clementine wanted to sink through the floor. Her pale skin flushed scarlet. Mr. Mildew sighed again.

"Well, that seems a reasonable enough motive. You can do a hundred lines by tomorrow: I must not dip little girls' hair in the ink. Try and use the correct apostrophe."

"Thanks squire." Ernie saluted. Shirley Temple wailed even louder.

"Gwendoline, is it?" drawled Mr. Mildew. "Stop that ridiculous noise. Go to the ladies room and sort yourself out. It's not as bad as the Blitz now, is it?"

"Gertie," he pointed at one of the Girl Guides, "make me a cup of sweet tea, there's a girl. I'm getting a swine of a headache."

Clementine glanced over at the dark-haired girl again who gave her an encouraging shrug and a smile.

Ernie slid back in beside her. "Honestly Ern! You keep showing us up."

"Well she was askin' for it."

Chapter 5

At break-time, after a Rich Tea biscuit - slightly soft - they were
turned out into the village square. It was drizzly cold. Ernie ran
off and edged in easily amongst the knot of boys who had found
a ball to kick around. Clementine tried to rub the horse poo off
the sleeve of her pink coat with a piece of blotting paper.

A little knot of girls had gathered around Gwendoline, like
starlings on a piece of cake. Their hands reached out to her wet
coils of spoilt hair. Clementine heard one of their trilling
voices say, "The Kraut's reading again – probably spy plans for
Hitler..."

They were looking at the dark-haired girl, who was sheltering
under the lych-gate to the churchyard. Clementine took a breath
and walked over to join her. The ivy cast dark shadows on her
pale skin. Clementine edged in next to her casually, as though
she were sheltering from the rain.

"What are you reading?" she asked. The girl held up Persuasion
by Jane Austen.

"I like your brother," she said. Her accent was thick.
Clementine felt a shudder and tried not to show her fear. The
girl sounded German.

She held out her hand like she'd been taught to do. "I'm
Clementine."

"Giesele," the girl said. Her face was taut and closed - looking.
"Yes, it's German. I'm German. I'm Jewish, before you run

away. Unless that makes you run away too. I'm classified as a 'friendly alien'."

"Jewish!" Clementine was delighted. "My best friend Ruby Bloom from home, is Jewish. She does tap and singing with me. I go to her house on Friday nights, for the candles and chicken. She lives in Golders Green where the Hippodrome is. And I've read Daniel Deronda. He's my second most favourite hero, after Mr. Darcy and Heathcliff, well, my third then.

Giesele laughed, but she looked really happy. The wary pinched look fell away. "That is one of my favourite books also." A robin settled on a branch of the yew tree and Clementine took it as a good omen.

"What did you say your name was? Giesele?"

"Yes, it's German for Giselle, like the ballet. My mother named me for that."

"I love Giselle! I danced one of The Wilis at my stage school."

"Me too at my ballet school! Do you have your pointe shoes?" Giesele asked.

"Yes, yes!" Clementine exclaimed. "We can practise together!" The two girls were jumping up and down, practically hugging each other by now, so relieved to have found a kindred spirit and both thoroughly delighted with themselves and their superior tastes.

The Girl Guides in blue, who were playing an elaborate skipping game, stopped and smiled over at them, beckoning them over to join the skipping. Clementine and Giesele rolled their eyes at each other. 'Skipping!' They called over, "No thanks!"

Gwendoline stopped the bossy game of, "Here comes a candle to light you to bed…" which she was organizing, to spit out something about, "German spies clubbing together" and changed the sing-song to, "Here comes a chopper to chop off your head chip chop chip chop… the last…KRAUT'S…dead!"

Gertie, the smiley Girl Guide who'd given Clementine the sweet tea yesterday, stopped mid jump and strode over to Gwendoline's procession of village children. She pushed aside the arch of children's arms which were about to bring the 'chopper' down.

"You little idiot." Gertie hissed at Gwendoline, "…Giesele is Jewish. Her whole family's been taken away by the Nazis, so why don't you just shut up."

The children fell silent. Gwendoline flushed pink and opened her mouth angrily just as the bell rang for the end of playtime.

Clementine looked at Giesele. Her face was closed and blank. "Do-gooders," Giesele said tonelessly.

She could see that Giesele hated to be pitied by the kind girls. She could understand that. "And they've got no style," Clementine said.

The girls walked back across the square towards the The Maypole, beneath a turbulent sky.

School stopped at three-thirty. Ernie had been told to write his hundred lines by tomorrow morning or he'd get, "Six of the best, on the bum with the slipper." As they were pulling on their damp coats Gertie and two of her Girl Guide friends came over.

"Don't worry, he hardly ever hits anyone. He's nice really. Try and write your lines very small so as not to waste paper or ink. We collect paper…for the war effort." Gertie held out her hand to Clementine and the other two introduced themselves as Olive and Molly.

"You could help too, you know…" said Gertie. "Collecting stuff and raising money. We have meetings in the village hall."

"And we go camping and have adventures," chipped in Molly. "Were you a Brownie, or anything, in London?"

The girls were friendly, which was a relief.

"I didn't really have time. I was at stage school. Acting and dancing and rehearsing for pantomimes and things," Clementine replied.

Gertie and Molly seemed really interested. Not just wanting to talk about themselves, like most girls did. Clementine smiled but she didn't feel all that keen on Guiding and all that outdoorsy business. For one thing, she didn't much like the idea of camping in wet tents and cooking on fires. And the only person she really wanted to think about, at the moment, was Giesele.

Chapter 6

Outside The Maypole, the granite sky threatened thunder. As
the children were bickering over how to share the bicycle on
the way back to Darkevaine House and who should have it first,
heavy, greasy drops of rain started to fall.

Ronnie tugged Clementine's sleeve. Giesele was waving to
them from the churchyard, where she stood sheltering under
the dark trees of the yew walk. A flash of lightning lit her up –
pale and beautiful amidst the gravestones. She was beckoning
them to join her and take shelter under the arch of trees.

They raced over the cobblestones of the square, as best they
could, wheeling the cumbersome bike and barking their shins
on it.

As they ran under the lych-gate Ronnie nestled into
Clementine's pink coat. "Is it haunted in here? I don't like it."

"Yes," said Ernie. "Yes it is... at night the corpses all climb out
of their coffins and graves and dance around wiv each other...
and when there's a thunder storm...the lightning wakes 'em
up..."

Clementine cuffed him. "Shut up Ern! Don't take any notice
Ronnie!"

Giesele laughed as she pulled them under the archway of trees
into the green, underwatery light where it was dry.

"They're all peaceful here... It's the living people you have to fear. Especially the girls. But maybe not too close to the trees in case of a, you know, a flashing ... blitz."

They all felt the shock of the German word, and its London meaning, run through them.

"A lightning flash" said Clementine quickly. "That's what it means."

"Sorry. Yes," Giesele flushed. "Come inside and shelter. This is where I live. You can get warm."

"You live in a graveyard?" squealed Ernie. "What, in a tomb?"

Giesele laughed again. "No, stupid! Over there!" She pointed to a gate with an arch of ivy over it at the end of the churchyard.

"There! In the vicar's house. The vicarage. Quite ironic for a Jewish girl, huh? Come and have tea. There is always cake. Proper cake made with eggs and butter."

At the mention of cake Ronnie and Ernie's faces lit up. They were all starving.

Outside the mulchy calm of the churchyard, came a sudden blast of singing from the village square – some kind of round-song, but modern and swinging. Clementine jumped, thrilled. An open, jeep-like truck came swaying fast through the rain. Three crew-cut headed soldiers in uniforms lounged in the back. Their booming voices were exciting as they sang: "I don't

know what's going on... you don't know what's going on... say
hi… hi"

"It sounds like a film," Clementine said.

"It's the GIs. The American soldiers", said Giesele.

"Yanks! Wow," said Ernie.

"They're down by the Bay…in a big camp or training place or
something. We don't know why. But it's something important.
People say it is something top secret. People here are very
worried about fifth columnists and spies. They're nice, the
Americans. The vicar's daughter goes out on dates with one of
them. They have music. And film magazines…they call them
movies. And real chocolate." Giesele explained.

Ernie watched, fascinated as the jeep and the singing swung
away into the rain and the square became quiet and grey again.
Clementine loved Americans. Not that she'd ever met one.
But she loved the idea of them: chorus girls and gangsters and
sparkling clothes and soda fountains and peroxided hair and tap
dancing. She felt an exciting shiver run through her.

They all jumped as another clap of thunder boomed and sent
them running through the archway of dark trees towards the
gate and the golden brick vicarage beyond it.

Chapter 7

Ernie and Ronnie sat in the vicarage kitchen, eating Mrs. Loam's walnut cake and fending off grown-up questions about Mrs. Milvaine, while the girls grabbed slices of cake and ran upstairs to Giesele's bedroom.

Giesele's room was prettily papered with roses and overlooked the churchyard. There was a cypress tree outside the window.

"Ooh you've got a window seat…do you lie here, gazing out at the melancholy scene, writing poems?"

Giesele laughed. On the dressing table was a heavy charm bracelet and a fine gold chain with a golden star on it. Clementine picked up the chain.

"It's a Star of David, isn't it? My friend Ruby's got one."

"We had to wear a yellow star sewn on our clothes at home. The Nazis made us. So everyone knows who are Jews. Who are Jews to shun. To spit at."

Clementine felt shocked but couldn't think of anything to say. Next to the bracelet, on a lace doily, was a bottle of perfume. "L'Heure Bleu," Guerlain, Paris.

"This looks delicious!" Clementine reached for the stopper on the intricate bottle. It was shaped like a hollow glass heart. Giesele took a step towards her. "Please don't touch it. It's my mother's."

"Oh. Sorry." Clementine blushed and turned away to the window.

The girls stood awkwardly in the odd light from the rain through the tree outside.

"Sorry," Giesele said.

"Show me your pointe shoes, then," said Clementine, throwing herself onto the flowery bedspread, luxuriously.

Giesele opened the old shiny wardrobe. As well as the glossy pink ballet shoes all sorts of strange and wonderful European things hung inside. There was a frothy violet party dress with a matching feather boa, which looked like something out of a Ginger Rogers and Fred Astaire film and a white tutu with a scarlet sash. And a suede coat, trimmed with white fur and a matching fur muff and hats and t-bar shoes and velvet skirts and an emerald silk shawl. Clementine picked up a bright pink scarf and held it up to her face.

"It's by Schiaparelli," said Giesele. "The colour is called 'shocking pink.' Beautiful with your hair, no?"

"Everything in the war is so brown and beige and mustard," said Clementine, holding up the bright scarf against her hair. "...and our friends in blue," said Giesele and they both giggled, Clementine following Giesele's lead.

Stuck in the frame of the mirror, inside the heavy cupboard

door, were some photographs. One was of a glamorous dark-haired couple sitting at a café table holding little cups.

The woman had a fur draped round her. Another photo showed Giesele herself with a big bow on her head with an older girl who looked like her but a bit sulky. They had a little dog, like a sausage.

Clementine felt Giesele tense up, "Your parents?" she asked… "They're so elegant. And who's that girl with you?"

Giesele pushed the wardrobe door shut. Her face closed up and Clementine felt as though shutters had come down.

"Klara," said Giesele coolly.

"Is she your sister?"

"Yes."

"Where is she?"

Giesele turned away again. The rain fell through the web of black cypress branches throwing dark shadows over her face. It felt like ages before she spoke again. "We came over together on the Kindertransport. The trains and boats they put Jewish children on to escape… from the Nazis. After we arrived in Harwich they sent us to a hostel in Norfolk to sort us all out. It was very cold. They couldn't keep us together. They sent me here. I write to her again and again at the hostel, but nothing comes back. I've heard nothing…"

Clementine was so shocked she didn't know what to say. She imagined Ronnie and Ernie disappearing suddenly like that, with her parents God knows where.

Giesele turned suddenly and crawled under the bed. She emerged, a bit dusty, with a mauve, oval suitcase, like a vanity case, and clicked open the lid. She flung magazine after magazine onto the bed. Heavy, shimmery-lidded, made-up faces cascaded onto the counterpane and stared moodily up from the satin.

"Moving picture magazines! You've got even more than me! I didn't know there were German ones! I've got hundreds of Picture Show and Film Weekly," Clementine exclaimed.

The girls settled comfortably onto the eiderdown with their pieces of cake, cut into tiny pieces to make the savouring last longer. They flicked happily through the glossy pages, lying side-by-side and exclaiming over the stars. Giesele translated extracts here and there.

"You look like Merle Oberon," Clementine said.

"You look like Myrna Loy," said Giesele.

"Do you think they're happy? They must be so happy, being so talented. With all those fans and everyone loving them. When you come over to my house, bring your pointe shoes and we can do some barre work together."

Clementine hesitated a moment and then spoke again.

"It's my birthday tomorrow. I don't usually tell anyone this, but it's the only special thing about me…and you've told me secret things about your family. There's this thing I'm going to inherit…It's called The Marchmont Chest. All the firstborn daughters in my family inherit it when they turn thirteen and then they put something in themselves and hand it down and no-one knows what's in it. My mother's aunt never had a daughter so it's coming to me. You must keep it a secret though…It never seemed that important before, but now I'm away from home… it really does. And well…it's arriving on my birthday."

Giesele sat up straight and her eyes shone. "But that is incredible. Your heritage. And your destiny! How long has it been happening?"

"I think since Henry the Eighth's time. He was this fat old king in the sixteenth century."

"Henry the Eighth! Brutal and fat tyrant! Six wives!" said Giesele, thrilled.

Clementine was really pleased she'd told Giesele about the chest. She seemed so impressed.

Clementine walked along the hallway of the vicarage looking for the bathroom. She stopped, even though she was longing for a wee. There was an odd tapping noise, insistent and urgent, coming from one of the rooms. As she peeked in, the door was gently, but firmly, kicked closed. She'd just had time to catch a glimpse of a long leg, a blue uniform and a flash of red lipstick.

When she got back to Giesele's room she asked, "What's that tapping noise at the end of the hall?"

"Yes I often hear it this week. That's the room of their daughter, Myrtle, I told you about. She's eighteen. She's quite mysterious. She's very friendly with the Americans at the military base. A high up one, called Rick, is her boyfriend. I think it's code they're teaching her."

Clementine felt a rush of excitement. "What sort of code?"

Giesele shrugged. "I don't know, but I want to find out, too."

Chapter 8

The storm had stopped and the air was chill, as the children
rode and trotted back to Darkevaine House. They were full
of cake and feeling much more cheerful than they'd been that
morning. The boys were chewing and Ernie held out a stick of
grey gum to Clementine.

"Where'd you get that?" she asked.

"Myrtle gave it us. It's American."

Clementine bit into the gum thoughtfully, working its floury
planes into a smooth ball. It tasted punchier than any she'd ever
tasted. It tasted like Hollywood and tap dancing in hotel lobbies
with shiny staircases…it tasted like danger and adventure. And
it made her think about the tapping noise in Myrtle's room.

After a rather dank supper of gristly stew followed by
blancmange, Mrs. Milvaine joined them to ask a few vague
questions about their day. It seemed to be a great effort for her.
She could only really concentrate on the animals. She let the
dogs lick the children's plates, which made Clementine gag,
and fed Merlin a spoonful of pink blancmange, which he licked
at disdainfully then left.

Ernie and Ronnie looked on longingly as Mrs. Milvaine laid
down her plate for Orion. Even though it was gristle, flavoured
with Bovril, they would have gladly wolfed it down themselves.
She got up and pulled open a sideboard. Inside were some old
board games: Scrabble and Monopoly and a puzzle of

Buckingham Palace. Ernie caught a glimpse of some quite tempting-looking soldiers, but she didn't take those out. She held out the boxes to Clementine.

"Here, take these, dear. It must be dreary for you… boys need games."

A wave of weariness passed over her face and she gathered up Merlin and called to the dogs.

"Thanks ever so, Mrs. Milvaine," said Clementine.

"You shouldn't say 'thanks ever so.' It's rather common and you have a lovely voice otherwise. You should say 'thank you very much'."

Clementine flushed. "Sorry. I mean thank you very much."

"Yes, well. Goodnight now."

Miss Smithers came to clear away. Anxiously, Clementine mentioned her birthday and that she might be expecting the arrival of the chest from lawyers in Devon and how worried she'd been that it would be lost at the station with no-one knowing her address. Smithers seemed kinder this evening and said she'd make the necessary arrangements and even smiled.

******

The children went up to Yellow Whiskers, carrying the boxes of games. They pulled on every layer of clothing they possessed, even though there was a small fire lit in the grate, which made the room a bit more comforting.

"She's a loony," said Ernie. "Ever so, ever so loony..."

"I think she's just very sad," said Clementine.

"Ever so, ever so sad?"

"The photos of the soldier...the schoolboy...the toys...and when I showed Miss Smithers Ronnie's sheet this morning..."

Ronnie shoved her, "Shut up!"

"Sorry Ronron, I'm just saying...I think her son must be in the war...that soldier's her boy... Imagine mum without us."

"Well, mum is without us," said Ernie.

The words hung heavy between them. Home thoughts running through them like cold water. Saturday morning pictures. Mum's Sunday roast. Dad's Woodbines.

Clementine opened out the scrabble board, they piled into bed and began to play a noisy, argumentative game.

"No, Ernie, Christmas is NOT spelt C R I S M I S!..."

After a while Ronnie asked, "So, cos she's sad, she only talks to the cats and dogs?"

"Well, maybe we make her feel more sad. We might remind her of things…"

All the children were thinking about Camden Town. Not even knowing whether mum and dad and the baby were down the Underground, sheltering. Or caught too late in a blast. Or the house bombed to a shell like a smashed-up doll's house. Clementine couldn't think of the right thing to say to comfort the boys.

Why was it so hard to talk about the important things, even when they're roiling in your guts? Instead, Clementine got up and turned off the light and pulled back the blackout curtains. The stars were clear in the inky sky.

"Same stars as at home. The Great Bear, Cassiopeia…" said Ernie – stars were his thing and Clementine knew they always soothed him, listing them, making a collection of them in his head like cricket statistics.

"Orion's Belt," said Clementine.

Ernie swiped her, "You always say Orion's Belt. It's the only one you remember."

"Is not."

Clementine closed the curtains and they settled under the covers.

"I can't believe it's my birthday tomorrow…"

But the boys were already snuffling on either side of her. She tried to take herself down with them into sleep, but her mind was whirling with images of the day. Giesele's sharp sad eyes; her sister Klara in the white dress and the horrors Ruby Bloom's uncle had said were happening in Berlin.

She couldn't turn off her mind: The Girl Guides kept popping up with their hopeful faces. They seemed to be the only ones who weren't lost, the only ones who knew what they were for... that tap tap tapping from Myrtle's bedroom... tap tapping...was she a spy?

She started thinking about what Giesele had said about the Marchmont Chest... She was right, it was exciting - her family's past. Mum's Aunt Connie had met Amelia Elliot who she'd inherited it from.

Amelia had been on the stage and had to get the chest back from a wicked uncle or something. Clementine wished she'd listened more when her mother told her about it.

Then Gwendoline's inky ringlet popped into her head.

The jolt of a missed step and she lurched awake... Oh heck... Ernie had forgotten to do his dratted hundred lines...

Chapter 9

The half-light filtering under the gap in the blackout was eerie and the air seemed even more hushed than usual. Clementine wrapped herself in a blanket and went to the window. In the dawn light the garden and the forest were ice white. It was like a melted Christmas cake. It had snowed. She shook Ronnie and Ern awake. They shrieked with delight.

School would be closed, surely! And Ernie would have a reprieve from his lines.

They got back under the bedclothes. Clementine sniffed dramatically and the boys remembered. "Happy Birthday, Clem!"

"Look what I got you!" Ronnie was pulling out a little package from under the pillow, wrapped in a drawing he'd done of Clementine with one leg, on school paper.

"Look it's you doing your dancing on your toes! Open your present, go on!"

Clementine smiled. She knew how mum felt now on Mother's Day pretending to be thrilled by cold burnt toast and greasy cards. She tore at the tissue: A bird skeleton.

"It's beautiful, Ronnie," Clementine exclaimed.

"I found it in the churchyard. All the spine is there and the head. I wanted to keep it myself really, but I knew you'd like it."

"I love it."

Ernie snorted and chucked a parcel over at Clementine.

"It's a Hershey's chocolate bar. It's American. Myrtle gave it to me yesterday. I might be able to do a few jobs for her," said Ernie casually. "Happy birthday, sis."

She threw her arms round both her brothers. Ronnie nestled in and slid his thumb into his mouth. Ernie shoved her off.

"Ugh get off. It's only a present." Ernie snorted.

Clementine ran down to breakfast hoping, hoping. And there it was - a card and letter and a little parcel from mum and dad, forwarded from the post office. She read the letter quickly to herself and then read it out loud. Hot tears started.

"Dearest Clemmie,
All of us at home are wishing a very happy birthday to our dear
big girl. Thirteen today! Baby Flo sends a sticky wet kiss
and next door's Mopsy sends a miao. She caught a sparrow last
night and left it on the step for me – you know how much I love
that!

We've been down the Underground to shelter twice this week
and Mrs. Cummins and her Agatha said they miss your singing.
Dad and Gran send a big hug to you and the boys. I know
you'll get Ronnie to wear both his vests and Ernie to change his
pants regular. I hope Ronnie hasn't been having his bed trouble
and that you've stopped the nail biting and that they're feeding
you your full rations, including meat. Especially the boys as
they need the meat energy. Maybe you could give Ernie some of
yours.

Well I better get the tea on and baby's nappy won't change itself, so signing off now Clemmie, my dear brave girl. Your ever loving, Mum xxx

PS The solicitor's letter is enclosed. How exciting! Tell me all about it in your next letter! Aunt Connie never would tell me what was in that dratted chest!

PPS Dad says many happy returns to his best girl."

The other letter was on stiff, creamy paper and it was from the solicitors in charge of the Marchmont legacy, telling them the time of the delivery of the Marchmont Chest from their offices in Exeter. They were putting it on the train to Oxbury. Miss Smithers, entering into the solemnity of the occasion said she'd arrange for Clinton to fetch it in the dog cart, if it could get through the snow.

Moths flittered in Clementine's stomach at the thought of the trunk. All those thirteen year old girls - her family, from strange Aunty Constance, all the way back to Henry the Eighth's time and her ancestor Matilda Marchmont. Her mum had longed all her life to know what would be in Aunt Constance's chest.

After gulping down their breakfast of toast, margarine and Spam there was a knock at the door. It was Giesele and the younger vicarage children and they were carrying skates. Miss Smithers called for Clinton and some ancient pairs of skates of varying sizes were fetched, cobwebby and mildewed, from the boot-room. Clementine wondered if they'd all belonged to Mrs. Milvaine's son as his feet grew through the years.

The little group walked excitedly through the crisp, smooth snow. None of the Harpers had ever skated before. But it was about balancing, wasn't it? It couldn't be harder than pirouetting in point shoes, could it? Giesele had a lilac fur muff slung round her neck, over her gas mask. Clinton appeared out of the stables and threw a wooly hat at Ronnie.

"Here. Keep you warm."

"Thanks ever so... I mean, thank you very much," said Clementine evenly.

Clementine noticed Clinton looking at Giesele and Giesele smiling back politely under her dark lashes. She found it a little irritating, though she wasn't sure why. Giesele linked her arm through Clementine's. "Happy Birthday," she smiled and thrust a little tissue-wrapped parcel into her hands. Clementine ripped it open to find the bright pink silk scarf.

Chapter 10

The lake was a cloudy mirror, opened like a lady's powder
compact, silver-edged and elegant, in the white woods.
Mufflered children were gliding about in the milky glare,
shrieking like gulls. Gwendoline was there, squealing
dramatically and clutching at three other girls.

Clementine lingered at the edge. She thought she would just
watch for a little while, but suddenly, Giesele crossed her arms
one over the other, grabbed Clementine's hands and slid her
onto the ice. "This is like a stage especially for your birthday
party, no?"

It felt free and frightening at the same time - to have and not
have control over her movements. But if she didn't think about
it too much she could do it. She let herself be propelled by her
friend. Giesele was smiling - pink spots on her pale cheeks, her
black cap of hair shining, like Snow White's, against the ice.

And then Myrtle arrived bursting onto the ice, wearing a bright
yellow hat, surrounded by a knot of American GIs. They all
skated around in a great gang, laughing and joshing and turning
the whole scene into a party. Or a number in a musical. They
encouraged the littler kids and laughed at a few cocky ones as
they fell over each other.

Clementine and Giesele were thrilled by the arrival of the
noisy gang, though they didn't say anything to each other. The
soldiers' easy laughter echoed around the frozen lake.

Clementine saw that Ernie was chatting quite casually to a
couple of the soldiers. Myrtle had called him over. They'd

brought chocolate with them and Ernie was holding another one of those Hershey bars he'd been showing off about. How could he be so bold! It was annoying.

A tall, black GI produced a pack of gum from behind Ernie's ear. She could tell some of the village children had never seen anyone black before and she felt like a sophisticated Londoner because, of course, she had. The soldier was showing Ernie a tricky skating move, sweeping down and then lifting him up high onto his shoulders.

Clementine longed to go over and be part of the show and yet she seemed to be stuck to the edge of the lake, resenting the others. Giesele's eyes were gleaming, a tiny silver lake reflecting in her black pupils. Myrtle had some sort of power. She shone. Clementine wondered how the specialness was connected to the secret tap tapping she'd heard in the corridor and seemed to hear it ticking inside her head again. Giesele had said Myrtle was a Sea Ranger. It was some sort of highest up thing after you'd been through the Girl Guides. And she had a proper, tight-fitting glamorous uniform.

Many of the Girl Guides saluted Myrtle and the American soldiers as they twirled and slid past, all thrilled to see her. Snatches of their eager cries sliced through the chill air. "We've collected lots of silver foil...", "Cotton reels coming on well, Myrtle...", "The planning committee...keep it hush, hush...". Then she saw Gertie and Olive skate over to Myrtle to tell her something. They were pointing over to Clementine and Giesele.

Clementine suddenly felt like she'd quite like to be one of the blue girls in uniform helping Myrtle. Knowing what they had to do. Helping with the war. Being important. Being part of a gang. Myrtle glided onto the ice and the GIs twirled with her and the Guides skittered about, around them.

Giesele whispered urgently in her ear. "Let's show the Yanks that we are something, too."

She pulled Clementine onto the ice and flew into an arabesque, arms outstretched – sleek and balletic. Myrtle and the American soldiers looked up and applauded. Gwendoline and the stuck-up London girls at the edge glared. Clementine followed and tried to imitate Giesele.

She started well, but her balance didn't hold and, as soon as she started thinking about what she was doing, she teetered and then fell spectacularly, ploughing right into the path of the black GI. He casually scooped her up, put her on her feet and saved her humiliation by making it seem like part of the fun.

"Woah there, Red! You just flew into my arms." His name was Chuck and he had bright, kind eyes.

******

Molly and Gertie skated over as she and Giesele were unbuckling their skates.

"Hello girls. That was a super move. I think Myrtle wants to talk to you about something," said Gertie, excitedly.

Clementine and Giesele tried to act casual as Myrtle swooped over in a wide figure of eight. Her scarlet mouth curved in an easy smile. "I didn't know you were an ice dancer Giesele. And you're Ernie's sister, aren't you? The stage school starlet?"

Clementine felt herself blushing. Was she being mocked? It didn't matter really, usually she didn't like teasing but Myrtle made you feel important and like a light was shining on you.

"We simply adore Ernie already. He's such a character!" said Myrtle. "Listen, we might have something you two can help us with. Why don't you come to the Guides meeting tomorrow? It's after school in the church hall. You see, we're planning a Christmas show. For the GIs, and to raise money for the war effort. We could do with some professional advice."

Clementine tried to bite back a glowing smile.

On the way home Giesele remembered she had to pop into the village shop for some Oxo cubes for Mrs. Loame. Clementine was longing to get back to see if the chest had arrived yet but stayed with her and sent Ronnie and Ernie on ahead.

"But don't you dare touch it if it has!" she warned them.

"I'm gonna see Rick and Chuck anyway" said Ernie casually. "You can come with me, Rons. As long as you don't suck your thumb."

The shop, which was also a post office, was the hub of the village. There were biscuits, tempting in glass-topped silver boxes. You could get a few broken ones for a penny.

Miss Pike the post-mistress stood behind the counter. Clementine recognized her as the fish-faced woman from the 'slave market' who'd asked if she had head lice. Her expression grew even more sour when she saw Giesele.

Gluey, peach lipstick gathered in the cracks above her mouth and there was a little smear of it on her front teeth. "Ah yes, Oxo. It stretches out the meat when you've got all those new foreign mouths to feed. I expect it tastes funny to you dear, doesn't it, our English food?"

Giesele replied impassively. "Not so funny, more disgusting, actually."

The woman's eyes narrowed sharply. Giesele's face was a perfect blank as she turned away.

"Sometimes I feel I am still wearing the yellow star on my coat," she said calmly as they left the shop.

"Well, I'd be proud to wear a yellow star," said Clementine. "You know who you are. I don't really know what I am, except I want to be an actress."

The Guides crowded in with loud dings of the shop bell and swarmed comfortably round the two girls. It was so easy for them to fit in. They look pleased to see Clementine and Giesele again so soon.

"Hello strangers! See you tomorrow at the meeting? Don't forget!" called Molly, over her shoulder.

Chapter 11

The girls raced home from the shop through the snow, pulled off their slushy wellies and piled up their skates. Ronnie and Ernie weren't far behind.

There it was already, waiting in the hall. The dogs were sniffing at it warily. Clementine stood and stared. It wasn't like the shiny treasure chest she'd been expecting. It was dark and treacly looking.

Miss Smithers, looking slightly flushed with the drama of it all, handed Clementine a creamy envelope. When she opened it, she found a tarnished silver key on a chain. Her hands shook a little as she put the key in the lock. All those girls before her, who had held this key, marched in a long procession through her mind.

The lock was stiff, but the key turned. Giesele came to kneel next to her as Ernie and Ronnie helped her heave up the lid.

A breath of scented air. Musty. Fusty. At first Clementine felt a rush of disappointment: no shiny jewels or precious stones. Lots of odd, crazily assorted things lay in a big tangle.

But Giesele gasped. "Oh this is incredible! Your family. Your history. All those girls and women like you! Can you breathe?" She was entranced.

This made Clementine feel excited again. Especially when Giesele reached in to pull out a polished box contraption, but suddenly Clementine almost wanted to slap her hand away. It was HER box. Giesele read out an instruction paper attached to it. " Fleet and Carlos' Most Amazing Magical Disappearing Machine. As marvelled at on the London Stage. Make your assistant disappear into thin air."

Ernie grabbed at it, without reading the instructions, pulled it upwards releasing a rusty lever and it flipped up into an extending cabinet thing. He got inside it. Nothing happened. He stayed inside for a moment, feeling rather silly then got out again and they all laughed.

Clementine pulled out an embroidered lace bridal veil, very old-fashioned looking, with a smear of blood on its edge.

"What beautiful lace! It's exquisite. Georgian or Victorian at least. Who do you think wore it?" Giesele gasped.

Giesele carefully unfurled the veil and, as she shook it out, found a dusty, diamond tiara was wrapped inside it. This was more like it! Clementine almost snatched it away as Giesele was starting to put both the veil and the intricate tiara on her dark shining head. Clementine could stand it no longer and pulled the veil and tiara out of her hands to try them on herself.

Then Ronnie pulled out a rotating metal, science-looking thing, which Ernie said was a gyroscope. There was an Indian feathered headdress and a skull… There was a battered, ancient leather journal written in old curly handwriting. *The most sacred and secret diary of Matilda Marchmont.* Clementine flipped through a few yellowed pages. The word "spy" leapt out at her and she slid it into her pocket to read later.

They pulled out a blue velvet cloak, which Giesele said was an opera cloak and a tiny china teapot and little cups hand-painted with birds...then a very old heart shaped brooch. "D'you think it was a love token!" Clementine exclaimed.

Giesele pulled out a large quilt, made of dozens of different embroidered octagons sewn together, each embroidered with pears and acorns and flowers and cats and in one corner an embroidered Indian girl with plaits and a feathered headdress.

"It looks American," said Giesele, thrilled, unfolding the quilt. "It's like it has a story on it..."

Her eyes sparkled as she found a worn out golden leather lace-up dancing shoe. Then a huge yellow silk umbrella. She wrapped the quilt round her shoulders. "If I had such a trunk from my family I would climb inside and go to sleep and breathe their air and return into the past with those girls and never come out again."

"Let's save the rest for later," said Clementine sharply, suddenly wanting to be alone with her past, making all the discoveries on her own. Her discoveries.

Clementine closed the lid. Giesele stood up, understanding immediately and flushed a little. Clementine got up and dusted off her skirt briskly.

"I might have a go with that disappearing cabinet. Work up an act," Ernie announced.

"I'll do it wiv you Ernie. Let me! Please let me!" said Ronnie. "I'm small so I could easily disappear."

"Well, I'd rather have a glamorous assistant, but I suppose you'd do to start off with. Rick and Chuck will love it. We can show them. Yanks love all that English, old Dickensy type of stuff."

"Alright. You can use the disappearing contraption with Ronnie, but you have to be careful of it. They're heirlooms. Everything has to go back into MY chest. For my descendents. My daughters. Anyway, I'm the performer in this family."

"Oh, stop showing off," said Ernie. "What would you have to leave in the mouldy old chest? Your nit comb and your spot cream? Maybe if you ever get big enough bosoms to need a bra, you can put that in it."

Giesele laughed.

"Who's going to want to marry you anyway, to have any daughters?" Ernie went on, encouraged by the laughter. Clementine threw a wellie at him screaming, "Shut up, shut up," until she started the dogs howling and Miss Smithers appeared to say it was time for her birthday tea.

All the children filed rather grumpily into the dining room but peace was restored when they saw that Miss Smithers had found extra powdered egg and some sugar and made a birthday cake.

Clementine smiled at Giesele trying to make up. "I'm glad you opened the chest with me. It's made my birthday even more special."

Clementine couldn't sleep. She didn't know why, but it made her feel strange, the whole Chest business. As though she didn't deserve it or wasn't grown up enough for it, or she didn't want to have to be grown up enough. Or something. And Giesele seemed to appreciate everything more than she did and knew about Georgian lace and history and things. She pushed the feelings away. She'd heard about it so often since she was little – Aunt Connie telling her about what her aunt Amelia had been through to protect it. She'd always thought she herself would be mature and sophisticated once it came to be her turn to inherit it. But what serious thing could she ever do to make a mark on the world?

Chapter 12

Through lessons the next day Clementine wondered about the Guides' meeting and the show for the GIs. Clementine looked at Giesele's closed face thoughtfully. She might have to push Giesele to go.

Clementine gazed at the clock throughout Geography, drawing smeary flowers on her hand as Mr. Mildew drawled on about stalagmites. After school, Clementine followed Giesele into the snowy graveyard.

"We're going, aren't we? To the church hall after tea?"

Giesele shrugged. "Maybe not."

"You said we would!"

"Well, now I don't know," said Giesele.

"Right," said Clementine infuriated. "Well, I'll go on my own, then."

"Alright. I'll come. Keep your hairs on!"

"It's not 'keep your hairs on'. It's keep your hair on!"

"Well, how much German do you speak?"

"None. Thank goodness."

"Hilarious. Sarcasm."

"Well, Germans have such a great sense of humour, don't they!" Clementine retorted.

"As you know, I'm a Jew and we're the funniest people in the world."

"Yes, you're always a barrel of laughs."

"Fine."

"Yes. Fine"

In Giesele's room, the girls lay on the bed, with pieces of bread and jam cut into tiny squares to make them into what Giesele called "petites fours", which were posh little cakes apparently. Though they were hardly fondant fancies. Clementine had once had fondant fancies for a treat at the Viennese café in Lyons Corner House in Piccadilly with mum, when they went shopping in the West End to buy her ballet shoes.

Giesele wasn't the only one to miss her mother, she thought. Then she felt guilty, remembering what might be happening to Giesele's parents if they were in one of those terrible camps that people whispered about. Concentration camps. But her own parents could be bombed any night in Camden Town. Shutters down, don't think about it, like Giesele does. Think something happy. All those dangerous words that mustn't be thought about, like blitz and shelter and barrage, marched through her mind.

"It could be fun being in a show again," Clementine said casually, anxious for Giesele to approve of the idea.

"Madame Pearl says you should perform whenever you can. And it is for the war. Performing for Americans… it'd be really fun, wouldn't it?"

She really wanted something to look forward to.

Giesele dunked her bread thoughtfully into her milky tea.

"I think it's not just about the show. It's not like you're famous or anything," Giesele said thoughtfully. "I think there's something else. Myrtle wouldn't bother with us unless it was something really important?"

"What do you mean? Like a mission? But we're not even Guides. She's got all those Guides dying to do missions for her," said Clementine.

"Yes but they haven't got what we have…" Giesele answered.

"What? Super talent and good looks? Brute strength?"

They both laughed.

"They can all light fires and shoot things and lay traps and make tents and fry sausages on sticks. And be brave and plucky," said Clementine. "She wouldn't need us for any of that stuff."

"No… but it must be something we have that they don't…"

"Please let's go to the meeting and find out," said Clementine, feeling quite desperate. "Perhaps the Americans, they might be able to help with... you know with... Klara... Please let's go. It's starting soon."

The shutters came down behind Giesele's eyes again and she didn't reply for a while.

Until she finally said, "Maybe."

The girls walked in sniffy silence through the cemetery and pushed open the door to the church hall. It was full of jolly chattering, which made them even grumpier. Some of the girls were wearing dyed shirts and homemade blue scarves made out of tea towels. So the Guides aren't just rich girls, Clementine thought.

Gertie and Pam and a couple of other girls came over, smiling, carrying a plate of custard creams.

"They're broken ones. Miss Pike gives us the stale ones in return for some sweeping and sorting, but they're still quite nice. Dig in!"

"So do we need to be good at camping and map reading and that sort of thing?" asked Clementine.

The Guides laughed.

"No! It's not just camping, though that is super fun. But we do lots of war work. We help in the hospitals as first-aiders and help the orderlies on the wards..."

"And we help on the farms with harvesting in the summer and we help doing the milking cos all the men are away on service," Gertie explained.

"And we collect tin foil and paper and..." said Pam.

"So... What about the show?" ventured Clementine, casually.

Pam leant forward. "Yes, well, we're holding a meeting for organizing the Christmas show. And we're a bit stumped for ideas."

"So far, Rita's going to recite "The Lady of Shallot," and we've planned a comedy skit about Hitler and Goebbels."

"That sounds hilarious,' said Giesele, deadpan. Pam flushed.

"Oh I'm sorry Giesele. Is that how you say it? I wonder if we might call you G? Might be easier."

Clementine and Giesele exchanged a look.

"Sure." Giesele said,

The Guides didn't quite know what to make of Giesele's mix of ironic tough shell and sensitivity.

"Anyway. So... the show?" prompted Clementine again.

"Oh yes. So what we need is a dance. A European ballet perhaps? Something sophisticated." Pam mused. "We wondered if you could choreograph it and dance it and teach the girls what to do. And maybe if you have any costumes, G? You always have such pretty and interesting clothes."

"D'you think American soldiers like ballet?" said Clementine doubtfully. "I think...maybe some tap dancing and singing, something modern like in a Hollywood picture?" she ventured.

"Super!" said Pam and Molly together.

A hush fell on the chirping room. Myrtle had arrived, dressed in her Sea Rangers uniform. A path seemed to clear for her. Myrtle greeted everyone and then swept Clementine and Giesele into a corner. The other younger girls saluted and looked deferential, bringing her a chair and a cup of tea.

Molly, Pam and Gertie, who were the next eldest, and seemed to be like her lieutenants, came and sat by them, bringing ginger nuts and efficient-looking reporters' notebooks. Pam stuck a pencil behind her ear.

Myrtle tossed back her hair. She was soldier-like and brisk in her uniform, but glamorous with her scarlet nails and lipsticked mouth. "Ok girls. As you may have guessed, we haven't just brought you here because of the show. It's something else. Something top secret. And it might be dangerous."

Clementine's heart sank. She wanted it to be about the show. Dangerous didn't sound tempting at all. She'd liked the idea of the sophisticated ballet and the Hollywood tap dance very much.

"We do want you to be part of the show of course," assured Myrtle.

"It'll raise loads of money for the war effort and entertain the troops and be a great cover for operations," said Pam and Clementine breathed again.

Myrtle leaned forward confidentially, "But I've got a real mission for you. I can't say too much about it, because it's hush, hush, but there's important training going on in the Yanks' base. There's a big operation to protect Tiger Bay. We can't tell you what. It's safer for you if you don't know too much."

Clementine felt thrills of importance running through her.

"So, here's the thing," Myrtle continued. "We've been given to believe that there may be a spy in the village or in the immediate vicinity, who's passing on information to the krauts. Sorry Giesele. The Germans."

Giesele flushed. "That is ok. I think you know I hate the Nazis."

"Absolutely. Point taken," said Myrtle.

She continued, "We've seen flashing, like some sort of signaling, coming from a window in the large house in the woods. It's a big old mansion that's recently been let to a new tenant. We can't break the code of the flashing, although we're trying. Rick has got his best people on it, but it makes no sense. It must be something very sophisticated - if that is how they're getting their info out."

"It's called Cerne House," said Pam. "We camped as near to

it as we could on our night camp last week, but the walls are really high."

"All we know is that there's a German woman living there," Myrtle continued. "We don't know anything about her. Her servant, an English butler, says her name is Mrs. Whitehead, in the post office. But it's common knowledge she's German. Everyone knows. It all looks very suspicious to us."

Molly and Gertie nodded urgently.

"She doesn't even have a char woman. The butler does all the work, so we haven't been able to get anyone in. Her accent is very strong. She gets parcels, really heavy ones, from Switzerland, though we think they originate in Berlin. They're addressed to her, as Frieda Whitehead."

Molly chipped in excitedly, "I managed to feel one of the parcels in the post office sorting section, when I was helping collect the tin foil for the foil rally, from Miss Pike. They were heavy and round - like heavy metal tins…"

Pam chipped in, as though Molly was taking a bit too much limelight. "But not cake tins, much slimmer than that and wide and flat and whatever's inside is really heavy and slides around a bit if you shake the parcels."

Myrtle leant forward, "So we thought as Giesele speaks German…but is one of us. On our side…" .

Giesele shuddered slightly.

"No-one else does, you see, even at the base and Rick thought…well, it was Myrtle's idea of course…as you're both performers you'd be able to go under cover together really convincingly," filled in Gertie.

"Like spies?" Clementine said. Myrtle smiled encouragingly. "Here. One of the girls took a picture of the so-called Mrs. Whitehead on her box brownie camera and we've had it developed." Myrtle handed it to Clementine and Giesele. "This is she."

"I took it actually," said Pam proudly.

"Yes. Well done, Pam. Good work", said Myrtle.

The girls looked at the small, blurry image of Mrs. Whitehead. She was wearing cats-eye-shaped glasses and had a dark lipsticked mouth painted in a cupid's bow. She wore a long fur coat with a little fox draped round her neck.

"So?" said Myrtle seriously, looking from girl to girl. "What do you say? This is your chance to make a mark – make a real difference to the war effort. To our fight against oppression."

Giesele looked at her and nodded gravely. Clementine was almost bursting with excitement.

Myrtle shook their hands and Gertie, Molly and Pam grinned
and made some notes in the reporters' pads.

Giesele peered at the grainy picture again. It was a troubled,
haunted-looking, mask-like face. A gloved hand clasped the fur
at her neck. There was something about the face. Something
familiar.

Chapter 13

Clementine and Giesele hurried back to the vicarage after the meeting. Their hearts ticked fast and they felt flushed, even in the icy cold.

Giesele mimicked the eager girls, "Super work Molly and Pam! Ooh, Thank you, Myrtle, first class, hush hush!"

Clementine laughed but they were both really excited.

"Let's go there now, before tea," said Clementine as they raced up the stairs to Giesele's room.

"What should we wear?" asked Clementine as Giesele threw open her wardrobe.

"Hmm. Something to disguise ourselves? Some kind of camouflage."

"Should we ask Myrtle?" said Clementine.

"No. Let's do it on our own. We're as good as those Guides. We don't need to know how to tie knots and light fires, do we? We'll use our intelligence."

They decided on long dark coats and sombre headscarves.

Giesele tiptoed into the kitchen and cut two pieces of bread and cheese and wrapped them in a tea towel. They pulled their headscarves down over their hair and set off into the dark afternoon.

The snow was frozen crisp and glowed like icing in the moonlight as they crunched their way through the woods towards the mansion.

They shivered a little as they stood in front of the padlocked high gates - the words Cerne House were spelled out in ironwork curls, wreathed with ivy. Clementine felt her heart punching about inside her ribcage.

They looked at each other and giggled. Their dark coats and patterned scarves made them stand out more than ever against the gleaming pallor of the snow.

"If we wanted to be camouflaged we should have worn wedding dresses," said Clementine.

"Come on then. Leg me up," whispered Giesele.

Clementine cupped her hands and pushed up against Giesele's foot so she could clamber over the high, stone wall. Then Clementine followed her over, dropping nimbly into the soft snow on the other side, only slightly winded.

They wound their way up the driveway leaving deep foot prints.

"We've not really kept our visit a secret, so far, have we!" Clementine whispered.

The tall trees circling the drive were forbidding, their bare branches overgrown with ivy and brambles.

"It's like Manderley in Rebecca. Quite romantic," whispered Clementine.

"Not so romantic if she has a gun."

"Do you think she might?"

"Well, the Nazis would have armed her, for sure," said Giesele. "...if she is a spy."

"Of course. And they have knives in their heels and cyanide capsules to commit suicide with if they are captured. I saw it in 'Forever Ours'."

Giesele snorted.

The house itself was a grand-looking, sprawling place, but probably built in the 1920s. They crept up to a window. There was a narrow gap in the blackout and, sure enough as they got closer, an irregular flickering kind of signaling through a crack in the curtains, was reflected as a shaft in the snow.

Light... dark... light dark... light, light dark...

Fragmented, darting shadows. It reminded both the girls of something. Something reassuring. Something they both loved. Being at the flicks, that was it! Watching a cinema screen in the dark. They both recognized it at the same moment. They crept closer to the window and knelt in the flowerbed and Giesele climbed onto Clementine's shoulders and looked through.

Giesele gasped.

"What? What is it!" said Clementine, impatiently, crouching under her weight. "Let me look now!"

Clementine scattered Giesele into the snow. She stretched up to the windowsill and peered through the gap in the curtains herself.

"Oh…blimey!"

A woman in a red velvet dressing gown was sitting on a sofa in the dark. Flickering on a screen in front of her was the huge mask-like face of a movie star. The face of the woman in the film… was her own face… The woman on the sofa was weeping softly whilst on screen the woman in a sparkling satin gown pouted and laughed seductively with her dark slash of mouth. The woman on the sofa's face looked sad and haunted as she watched her beautiful, younger self…

The woman on screen held a glass of champagne. The woman on the sofa waved a cigarette holder, its end was carved like a snake's head, with a black cigarette. She sat by the shaft of the projector beam, lit up by the cloud of smoke wreathed around her. Clementine was mesmerized.

A man entered carrying a silver tray. He started walking towards the window, as though he'd seen the gap in the blackout. Clementine's blood froze and she slid quickly down below the windowsill. The girls shrank down low against the wall in the frozen shrubbery, quaking with tense excitement.

"I know her. I thought I recognized Pam's photograph. It's her!" Giesele hissed.

"Who?"

Giesele's face was flushed. "Shush. Come on. They might hear us!"

They ran back through the ghostly, thorny garden, stumbling over roots. Clementine was panting behind Giesele. As they leapt down into the snow on the other side of the gates, she started wheezing out questions.

"What is she? Who is she? Was that her on the screen? Tell!"

But Giesele just ran on and on, eyes glittering, until they got back to the safety of the vicarage.

Chapter 14

The girls flopped down onto Giesele's bed. Clementine punched Giesele's arm. "Tell! Tell, you beast!"

"I know her. The woman. I know her."

"Mrs. Whitehead?"

Giesele dropped to the floor and tugged the lilac valise out from under the bed. She threw the film magazines onto the bed and rifled through the pages of Glamor and Kurier.

"Look!"

A heavy-lidded, painted diva in a satin gown, holding a snake-headed cigarette holder. Under the picture, the name. 'Frieda Weiss.'

"It's her." exclaimed Geisele.

"A film star? Here? A real movie star?"

"Yes. And she's definitely not called Frieda Whitehead."

Clementine grabbed the magazine and scanned it eagerly.

"But could she be a spy, too?"

"She was in some films that Hitler liked," Giesele said thoughtfully. "He didn't ban them anyway. He likes actresses.

She could be working for the Nazis. Maybe she was watching herself up there in her own films and weeping about the fatherland. She looks very blonde and Aryan."

"What's that?" Clementine asked.

"Hitler's ideal white and blonde and blue-eyed 'racially pure' person."

"Yuck. But the flickering...it wasn't...Morse code, or any communication code. We saw that. It was just the film projector."

"Yes so...maybe she's sending the messages another way," Giesele said.

"Well, we'll find out how. Let's try and get into the house."

"We'll need to have a good story for getting in."

"We can say we're fans...well, we kind of are," said Clementine, getting excitied.

"Hmm...yes, I suppose she is a good actress," said Giesele.

"We can say we found out who she is. That we recognized her from your Kurier magazines and that you loved her films in Germany and that we wanted to meet her...and then we can see what we can find out."

"How could we ever get to have a look around? That butler sounds like a bodyguard," Giesele said. "We'll have to get on his good side, too."

"We can ask her to help with the Christmas show! And we can take autograph books and her picture from Kurier. I want an autograph anyway."

"You want an autograph? Even if she's a spy and a traitor and a Nazi?" said Giesele in disbelief.

"Well…why not! She's still a famous star. It'd stop Ernie showing off about his baseball player, supposedly big-deal autograph, and all his American mates and their chewing gum that he won't share."

"If you swallow American chewing gum it sticks inside your lungs. If you do it more than three times you can't breathe and it kills you," Giesele said.

"Really!?"

"No, not really, you idiot," said Giesele. "Maybe it's probably good if we can act like fans anyway. Safer for us."

"Frieda Weiss. We're your number one fans," drawled Clementine in an American accent.

"And she won't be able to say no to helping with the show because that would make her seem like a suspicious traitor."

"Yes, we can make her prove she's not dodgy by having to help with the show! We'll go back tomorrow after school. She probably stays up all night and sleeps all morning."

Clementine was thrilled. "Yes, we can go tomorrow!"

The girls were hugging each other and practically jumping up and down on the bed with excitement now. To think their lives had seemed so boring and hopeless just a couple of days ago.

Chapter 15

That evening, Ronnie and Clementine were huddling by the fire in Yellow Whiskers, trying to dry their wet pullovers and socks over a chair. They were caked with ice after half an hour of excited snow-angeling in the lawn while huge snowflakes fell around them like paper doilies.

There was the sound of a motorcycle on the snowy gravel outside. A voice called out, "Bye, Kiddo!" and the bike buzzed off again. Ronnie peeled back the blackout at the window and looked down.

"Ern's just got off the back of Chuck's motorbike. Not fair!"

Ernie came galloping up the stairs, whistling casually and thumped in, cocky and damp and smoke-smelling and full of secrets and confidences. His pockets were full of what he called 'candy', which turned out to be sweets. Clementine thought she was meant to be the one with the mysterious new friend and enticing secrets. He was maddening.

"Where've you been all this time, Earnest Harper? Tell!"

"Wouldn't you like to know! There's things a guy can know and a gal can't. Interesting things."

He opened up a brand new film magazine with Rita Hayworth on the front cover and started whistling, smugly mysterious. Clementine lunged at her brother, roaring. She knocked him onto his back on the hearth-rug and clamped herself on top of his chest with her hands pinning him down. Looking down at him, with her face poised three inches from his, she said threateningly. "I'll spit right in your eyes if you don't tell me what you know."

Ernie struggled from side to side furiously but Clementine was strong from her ballet training.

Ronnie looked wide-eyed at the huge sweets that were rolling out of Ernie's pockets like marbles.

"Talk!" snarled Clementine. She let a bit of spit hang from her lips, threateningly.

"Alright – alright, keep your hair on," said Ernie.

"I went back to their base. They're training for a top secret thing. Really big. Hush, hush. That's why we've got to be very careful of fifth columnists. Like they have in Norway."

"What's filthy colonists?" asked Ron,

"Spies," said Ernie. "Traitors."

"What do you know about spies, you silly kid," said Clementine.

"More 'n you, stuck with your friend not knowing no-one. There's more going on, right under your noses, over at the vicarage if you had yer eyes open," said Ernie mysteriously.

"Our eyes open under our noses?" sneered Clementine.

"And kids can do a lot you know. Kids are very useful…that's what Rick says. Kids can get in all sorts of interesting places. Find out all sorts of interesting things," Ernie said smugly.

Clementine sat up thoughtfully and let Ernie roll away to a safe distance.

"Getting heavier since you stopped the dancing, aren't you, fatty!"

Clementine reared up again, snarling. Ronnie jumped between them.

"No more fighting, I want sweets."

******

That night Clementine's mind raced between the show and the film star recluse. Her boring life had suddenly become so exciting. She sat up in bed reading by torchlight after the boys were asleep. Matilda Marchmont's journal…she had been launched into an adult world at the age of thirteen, too.

At school the next day, Clementine sat next to Giesele and whispered, "D'you think we should tell Gertie and Molly about Frieda at break time?"

"No. I didn't see Myrtle at breakfast this morning. We must wait and tell Myrtle first," said Giesele.

"Or they'll get all our glory," said Clementine.

Giesele laughed because that was exactly what she'd meant. "I want to keep it just to ourselves for now, anyway. Til we find out more."

"Alright, and I had another idea," whispered Clementine. "We could use the things in the chest for the show. It'd make me sort of part of it. And maybe I'll do something brave that I could put in one day."

Mr. Mildew rapped on their desk with a ruler and they jumped. "Care to tell the whole class what's so interesting, girls?"

After school, lying on the high bed in Yellow Whiskers, the girls went through their plan again. Giesele brought out the copy of Kurier Magazine with the photo of Frieda Weiss in it and a chic autograph book.

"It's only got my teachers and friends in it and an opera singer who was a friend of my mother's. D'you want to sign it? You're my best friend now," Giesele said.

Clementine flushed. "And you're mine," she said.

******

The girls trudged through the slushy snow, arm in arm against the cold, on their way to Cerne House. They were whispering excitedly and giggling.

"We can tell Miss Weiss about the costumes in the chest."

"…if she lets us in."

"I feel a bit sick about being near an actual possible Nazi spy.
D'you think we'll be able to tell by the look of her? Or the
smell of her? I might faint," said Clementine

"Well, how do you think I feel about it? You always make it
a drama about you," snapped Giesele. "…Sorry, I am mean
sometimes. I feel scared and I don't want to feel like that."

"Of course you feel scared. We both do. I just think we could
treat it like a part in a play. An adventure. To make us feel
brave…"

Giesele smiled. "Yes, it's a good idea. You have good ideas."

As they hurried down the icy drive, past the stables, Clinton
came out, whistling casually. He chucked Clementine a parcel
and walked back inside.

Wrapped in newspaper was a copy of Modern Screen movie
magazine with Myrna Loy on the cover. It was only a few
months old. Myrna Loy had bobbed red hair like Clementine's
own. She blushed. Flipping cheek. But a copy of Modern
Screen…he must've got it especially from the Yanks or got
Ernie to get it for him.

Giesele nudged her. "He likes you, I think."

"Don't be daft!"

Chapter 16

They pulled a gap in the ivy-choked hedge next to the stone wall surrounding Cerne House, squeezed themselves through it, then trudged through the snowy gravel up to the heavy front door. There was an ornate bell-pull. Giesele grabbed it and gave a confident tug.

The butler, Mr. Carter, opened the door. He looked wary and tired.

"We're here to see…Mrs. Whitehead."

"I don't know how you got in here, but this is private property and I don't believe you've been invited," he said. He had a posh English accent.

Clementine put on her best Shirley Temple smile.

"Oh please. We know it's a frightful cheek but we've found out, you see…we know that Frieda Weiss lives here and we're enormous fans of hers and we promise not to tell a soul of her identity."

"We'd give anything for an autograph," Giesele added.

"I'm afraid I don't know what you are talking about but I will pass on your good wishes to Mrs. Whitehead. Good day to you girls."

"Could we just leave our autograph book?"

Mr. Carter took in Giesele's accent. "You are German?"

"Yes."

High heels clicked across parquet floor. A voice called from the shadows.

"Carter? What is it?"

"Some girls from the village, Madam. They're just leaving."

Giesele pulled Clementine's hand and tugged her boldly across the threshold, past the butler and into the hallway.

Giesele started to speak. "Please excuse our intrusion. We know who you are and we just worship you, Fraulein Weiss. I've seen all your films in Berlin. Many times."

"Come. You may come..." said Frieda Weiss

The woman retreated into the shadows of the fire-lit room beyond and the girls started to follow her, before Carter could stop them.

"Carter...let them come."

Frieda Weiss had retreated to the other side of the vast room. It was the one they'd seen through the curtains. It was dimly lit now, with golden light from table lamps, falling on lush rugs and plump brocade cushions. Clementine felt as though she were stepping onto a film set for an Arabian Nights Palace.

As the actress stepped into a pool of light, Clementine almost gasped. She was wearing a silver dressing gown and high-heeled slippers with feathers frothing at her ankles. Her face was pale and hollow beneath high cheekbones.

She was beautiful, but much older than she looked in her pictures in the magazine. She wore charcoal-like make-up round her eyes and had long blood-red nails.

"Come further forward, child. The one who knows Berlin."

Giesele stepped forward.

"So you are German. Why are you?...Ah you are..." Giesele flushed, "Yes...I am... a Jew."

"Ah, that terrible man. Terrible..." Frieda's voice seemed to soften.

"Liebling...you came all this way in the snow just to ask for an autograph?"

Giesele pulled Clementine into the pool of light with her. They stood together awkwardly.

"Ah. The other one has red hair. It is beautiful. You will like it when you are older."

"This is my friend Clementine. She wants to be an actress."

Frieda sang in a mock lamenting voice - that song again: "Oh my darling Clementine...She is lost and gone forever.

Does everyone sing that to you?"

Clementine nodded politely.

"That must be tedious. Why do you like to act?"

"Well, I want to be like Barbara Stanwyck and Myrna Loy. And you, of course…It's my burning ambition. I'm at stage school."

"Stage school. Oh dear," Frieda laughed. "Well, never mind."

Clementine flushed.

"May I offer you a Martini? Cigarette?"

The girls weren't sure if she was joking. They smiled uneasily as she lifted her own glass – triangular with an olive in a clear drink that looked like Gran's gin. She slid a black cigarette into the snakes-head holder.

Frieda Weiss laughed at them again. They couldn't be sure if it was a kind laugh or not. She started to hum "My Darling Clementine" under her breath.

"Funny girls."

The girls perched nervously on the edge of a silk sofa, anxious not to sit back and be consumed by the soft cushions. Clementine nudged Giesele in the ribs, then launched in herself,

"Actually…we have an enormous favour to ask you, Miss Weiss…you see…" she trailed off.

Giesele chimed in, "Yes…you see... we're helping the local Girl

Guides - quite boring girls - put on a show for the American GIs, at the base here, for Christmas…and to raise money for the war effort."

"And we wondered if you might consider…that is in any capacity, advise or, if you might… or even possibly perform a tiny cameo appearance or… anything really." Clementine's words dried up.

She felt sweat pool in the arms of her jersey, in the hot room. It smelt of orchids and perfume – like the strong scent Madame Pearl wore to shows.

Frieda Weiss didn't speak. Her face hung mask-like in the smoky air. Emotions flittered across it briefly: guilt; opportunity; duplicity; irritation; longing. Clementine didn't know how to decode them. She could have been thinking any of those things, or all of them, or none at all.

Frieda Weiss exhaled a plume of blue smoke before she spoke again. "You wish me to perform in your show?"

The girls nodded vigorously.

"I know that everyone in the village hates me. They know I'm German. Of course they do. What would happen if they find out who I am? That I am a star."

"But that's exactly it. It would be your chance to show them that you're a… good German," blurted out Clementine. "And how talented you are and that you want to help us win the war and that you don't want to help Hitler."

A charged silence. Clementine blushed. She wanted to sink into the floor.

"I am very tired, girls. Please leave now."

She turned away, out of the light and took another cigarette from a silver box.

The girls made for the door across the expanse of polished parquet, feeling like they ought to curtsey, feeling they'd failed miserably.

Frieda Weiss spoke again. "Come back tomorrow. I will give you my answer."

Hearts beating wildly they reached the hallway and exchanged a glance. Mr. Carter was standing tall and protective in the shadows. Clementine had the feeling that he'd been listening at the door the whole time.

The girls ran through the dark woods, stopped in the middle to scream with pent up hysteria, then hugged each other and jumped up and down beneath the snowy trees. Their words tumbled out.

"She's so strange!" squealed Giesele. "And rude!"

"Is she a spy? Is she mad?"

"... and she's so old - how old do you think she is?" asked Clementine.

"And she's also quite amazing. So does that mean she might be a spy?"

"We did it! We did it!" yelled Clementine.

"She still might say no!"

"No. She wants it. I know she does!"

"I really don't know if she's bad or not," said Giesele. "How can you tell if someone is evil? Spies are like actors, aren't they? And she is an actor. She is weird but sort of fabulous so maybe that makes her a spy."

"But if she does agree to do the show does that make her not a spy or is it a really clever cover?"

"We need to find Myrtle," said Giesele

"We need to debrief!" giggled Clementine.

"Ha-ha now we're real spies. Debrief! We sound like Molly and Pam!" Giesele declared.

They were so elated, they started a snowball fight and then ran back, flushed and wet, laughing to the vicarage to find Myrtle.

Chapter 17

As they let themselves into the vicarage they could hear music coming from the sitting room. The Loames had a gramophone player and a swing song was playing - Glenn Miller's "Blue Orchids." Myrtle was alone, dancing. She turned shiny-faced as the girls knocked and came in shyly.

Myrtle pulled Clementine towards her by her hands and twirled her forwards and back in a new American swing dance move. It was the kind of thing the GIs had been larking about with on the ice. Very modern and very exciting. Clementine, quick to pick up steps of course, imitated Myrtle and swung forwards and sideways with her and then scooted right through Myrtle's legs on the polished floor.

They flopped onto the sofa laughing.

"We have information...intelligence," said Giesele solemnly.

Myrtle sat up quickly, "Let's go up to my room."

Clementine was surprised to see how untidy Myrtle's room was – books, stockings, girdles and bras were strewn on chairs and on the bed, and the dressing table was laden with bottles and smeared with lipstick and face powder. She had imagined it would be more of an official control room with a radioing, signaling station and files and maybe a blackboard and a pointer.

Myrtle swept some books and knickers off a chair and they sat down on the bed.

"We've been to Mrs. Whitehead's," said Clementine dramatically.

"Did you get inside?" asked Myrtle.

"Yes. Well, not at first. We went at night, in camouflage, sort of. And then we made a plan and went back again today and then we did... get inside."

"We found out who she was first, too. I recognized her!" said Giesele. "Go on!" Myrtle was impressed.

"She's actually called Frieda Weiss and she's a film star in Germany. The flashing was a projector playing her old films. She sits there, in the dark and watches herself on a little screen," said Clementine triumphantly.

"Goodness! Well done!" Myrtle exclaimed.

"We posed as fans, trying to get an autograph and then I had a brainwave. I asked her...."

"Yes...well, we both asked her. It was sort of my idea the fan thing...we made the plan together," interrupted Clementine.

Giesele glared at her and Myrtle smiled. Ugh, Clementine realised – they'd become exactly like Pam and Molly trying to impress Myrtle.

"You've both done excellent work...go on!"

"Well, we thought…we both thought – as a way of going back and doing more investigation, we would ask her to be part of the show... to be in it…" said Giesele.

"Oh my goodness, a potential Nazi spy in the Christmas show!" said Myrtle.

"Did we do wrong? She sort of got carried away," said Clementine.

"Yes, we both did."

"Yes, we both got carried away. We knew we had to have a reason to be in the house more, so we said she'd have a chance to prove to the village that she was a good German. It was quite hard to try and convince her…"

Clementine and Giesele waited anxiously, pulses racing, a bit disappointed.

Myrtle creased her brow.

"No actually, I think it's rather brilliant to try and flatter her, gain her confidence and then to be actually working with her on the show. Absolutely brilliant. We can observe her and when she lets anything slip we can strike. You know we must be very careful not to reveal anything from the American base."

The girls nodded seriously, delighted.

"Anything at all. You see, someone is transmitting to Germany at eight o clock every evening from somewhere near the village."

"What sort of transmissions?"

"We're trying to break the code. It's some new German system."

Clementine thought of the mysterious tapping coming from Myrtle's room. Was that code-breaking then?

"And I suppose when you do break the code then it would be in German - the actual messages?" Giesele said.

Myrtle nodded. "Exactly."

"What are the Americans doing down there? What sort of training is it?" Clementine asked.

"I can't tell you…Better if you don't know," said Myrtle. "So let's plan your next move very carefully. You know, it might be very dangerous for you."

"Miss Weiss said we should go back tomorrow and then she'll give us an answer about being in the show," said Giesele.

"She might say no, but at least we can get another look round downstairs. Her butler – he's English - called Mr. Carter, he's really protective of her," added Clementine

Myrtle smiled. "Excellent. Really well done…Report back after tomorrow then."

Clementine felt her face shining. Giesele looked unusually happy, too.

Chapter 18

That night, in bed, when the boys were asleep, Clementine read more from Matilda Marchmont's journal. She was beginning to get more used to the faded twirly handwriting. "The most sacred and secret diary of Matilda Marchmont..." A phrase stood out. "I am a spy,... hiding in the shadows..." So had Matilda been a spy too? She couldn't trust anyone at King Henry's court. She didn't know who was good and who wasn't. She was away from her home and her parents, caught up in a complicated, dangerous, grown-up world. Clementine's heart started to race.

The snow had melted overnight and the ground beneath their bedroom window was a slush of dirty, eggwhitey peaks.

Miss Smithers had asked the children to help Clinton mend some fencing in the paddocks behind the stables. They'd been given some work clothes, cut down to their sizes. Clementine felt a bit like a farmer in her dungarees and sturdy boots, but she knew that girls and women had to help out on the land while the estate workers and farmers were at war. Myrtle and all the Guides helped out on the land. So she was a Land Girl and a spy now. She felt rather heroic as she hacked up a bit of tree root that was growing in the way of the fence posts. It was all very good experience for being an actress.

"Why're you looking so pleased with yourself?" asked Ernie.

Clementine just smiled to herself. "None of your beeswax."

"I don't care, anyway. I'm off down the base to meet Chuck and Patch."

"Well, they might be very grateful to me some day," said Clementine mysteriously.

Ernie ignored her. "Come on Ron! Let's get the disappearing cabinet and practise before I go."

He whistled up Orion, the border collie, to follow them. Clementine watched them go. Her muddy brothers seemed like a couple of country boys themselves now. Clinton was even going to teach them all to ride Hercules.

Giesele arrived after lunch - Spam sandwiches again. Both the girls were restless and excited as they left Darkevaine House, bundled up in their coats and head-scarves. They made their way up towards the woods on the other side of the vicarage. They didn't want anyone in the village to know where they were going, but as they passed the post office shop they saw Miss Pike peering suspiciously at them from behind a pyramid of tinned peas.

The gates of Cerne House were open, as though they were expected, and they pulled more confidently on the bell this time. Mr. Carter opened the door and ushered them, rather graciously, into the red velvet drawing room again. Miss Weiss was standing in the centre of the room, smoking a black cigarette. She beckoned them towards her, "Come."

The actress turned and they followed her through another door at the far end of the room. It led into another anteroom and she pushed open two double doors beyond. The girls didn't know what to expect. What if she was going to produce a gun and trap them? She might try to hold them prisoner in a basement. She might torture them for secrets. Clementine's heart raced.

Frieda pushed at the heavy double doors until they opened to reveal a huge, glittering ballroom. She switched on a crystal chandelier, dripping with glass droplets and the room was flooded with light.

"We could seat a hundred people and put a small stage at the end," said the actress.

She turned to see their excited faces.

"You cannot rehearse here, but you may hold the show here. I will rehearse my section, with you alone, here once. My performance will be a surprise for all the audience on the night."

The girls started stammering out their thanks.

Miss Weiss interrupted, "But you must tell them all, I am not a lover of Germany and that is why I left. I want to help the soldiers and the British war effort... and the Americans. I hate what is happening at home. I am ashamed."

Her eyes locked with Giesele's. Could they believe her?

The girls nodded. "Of course," said Clementine, who couldn't stop herself doing a small slide along the polished wood. "It's a sprung floor!"

"Of course it is, silly child. It is a ballroom," said Frieda curtly. "You will have to find chairs."

"Lots and lots of chairs!" said Clementine excitedly.

"The Girl Guides can collect chairs. They love to collect things!" said Giesele.

All three of them sniggered a little at this.

The mask-like face moved, shifted almost imperceptibly. If you moved closer to her you'd see fine lines laced beneath the powdery sheen of her face. But still she didn't quite smile. Briskly, Frieda Weiss turned away and closed the shutters on the nearest window. Everything she did was odd and laden with mysterious significance somehow. If only Clementine could read what it meant. If only she weren't so thrilled by her. "Carter will help you with arrangements…and such things…He is a very British, patriotic and also practical, man."

They were clearly being dismissed. Clementine curtseyed automatically.

"Stage-school child. You are so funny."

Clementine blushed.

Frieda Weiss stood beneath the chandelier and lit a cigarette. She waved goodbye to them with two emerald-ringed fingers, through a plume of smoke.

******

Clementine and Giesele said goodbye politely to Mr. Carter, who smiled much more kindly at them, and walked in a dignified way along the drive. But once they were out of the gates, they ran giggling through the woods again. They couldn't stop laughing for sheer triumph and at the weirdness of the whole situation.

"Stop! I'm going to wet my knickers!" shouted Clementine.

"Leetle stage school child you are zo fuuuny," Giesele mimicked Frieda's intense, Garboesque drawl.

"She's crackers."

"Bonkers!"

"But I still don't know if she is…she is one though... an evil spy?" said Clementine. "I don't know, do you? Why was she saying what a patriotic butler she has? I don't know what to think."

"How do you ever know who you can trust?" said Giesele. "I feel like I'm in a movie myself now," said Clementine.

"You always act like you're in a film or a play a bit, don't you," said Giesele.

Clementine bit her lip, stung. "Well, I don't think that's fair." Giesele was mean sometimes. "You're the one who's always acting the tragedy queen."

The girls turned their backs on each other. Clementine spoke first. "Sorry."

"I'm sorry, too," Giesele said.

"I mean this is important. Dangerous and important. I never did anything important before. I mean shows feel like they're important…" Clementine ventured.

"But this actually is about people dying. Being betrayed. People really are dying…" Giesele said.

Clementine flushed. It felt like Giesele was telling her off again and that was just what she was trying to say herself…she felt cross again and didn't feel like trying to put her feelings into words and getting sniped at again.

"Come on, we'll be late for the meeting and we have to go to the shop first." Clementine walked on ahead, through the biting chill air, towards the lights of the village.

It was annoying that they'd had another argument again because it had been a fantastic coup and she was dying to tell Myrtle what had happened. Thanks to them, they'd have access to Frieda Weiss's house. Why did things always seem to blow up between you when you liked your friend better than anyone?

Giesele linked her arm through hers. "I'm sorry. My feelings are not in a straight line sometimes. They are up and down and then up."

Clementine did understand. And she also thought that it was much better with Giesele than with people who pretended everything was happy and perfect all the time.

Giesele started to speak in a rush of words. It was easier when they weren't facing each other, "I am hard sometimes, I know. I wake up every morning and my face is wet from crying. I dream I am with them, my parents and Klara just doing something normal like having breakfast or shopping and then I wake up and I don't know where I am. I don't know where they are. But I can see a very dark place. A place very full of death... without hope. You don't need to say anything. Please don't."

Clementine squeezed her arm. Her own heart so often felt full of dread. It's not just me that feels terrible things, she thought - other people do too. How odd she thought, that she hadn't really realised that before.

Chapter 19

The girls reached the village shop and banged their hands
and feet to warm themselves up. Clementine had to buy some
darning thread for Miss Smithers. There was Mr. Carter again.
He had drawn up on his bicycle outside the post office and
came in greeting people cheerily. Surely he wouldn't work
for a spy? He approached the post office counter, laughing
charmingly with Miss Pike. She took a small parcel from him
for the post and then handed over a wide, flat one addressed to
Frieda.

Clementine whispered to Giesele excitedly when she saw it.

"I know what the round parcels are! It's the cans of her films.
They come in round tins. The films are on celluloid. I've seen
them stacked up in the projection room at our cinema. In
Camden."

"Oh yes," Giesele whispered back. "I've seen them too, in
Berlin. So does that mean they're not spying packages?"

"Well I suppose so, unless they're hidden in the films...Which
is possible..."

Miss Pike, smiling to reveal her large yellow teeth, produced a
box of chocolate biscuits and a shiny tin of tobacco. A proper
posh-looking one from before the war.

"I kept this for you, Mr. Carter, I know you like a proper
gentleman's smoke. I only keep it for my special customers."

Mr. Carter tipped his hat to Miss Pike and a mottled blush

spread over her whiskery cheeks. Clementine supposed he did have a bit of a Clark Gable look about him, with his dark mustache, but he was very old - at least thirty. He tipped his hat politely to the girls too and winked, as if to say how ridiculous the fish-faced woman was. "Fancy seeing both you ladies again so soon."

Giesele was looking at the dress patterns as Clementine went up to pay for the thread. Miss Pike sighed.

"He's a real gentlemen, that one. I don't know how he can bear to work for a Kraut..."

She paused and a sly smile twisted her thin lips, "Oh, sorry dear, I forgot - your friend's one, isn't she." She lowered her voice to a nasty whisper. "Well, almost worse than one, in a way, isn't she? That's what started Adolf off...those Jews."

Clementine was so shocked she threw the thread down on the counter and pulled Giesele out of the shop. She was furious at herself for not saying anything to the ghastly woman. Tears of frustration flooded her eyes.

Giesele laughed. "What was she saying? More anti-Semitic stuff? It doesn't worry me."

But Giesele's mouth was in a tight line as she started walking briskly away.

They passed Mr. Carter as he was putting on his bicycle clips.

"What a stupid woman. It's better to feel sorry for such ignorant people." He slipped the box of posh chocolate biscuits into Clementine's basket. "Share them with your friend while you're writing the show. Creative minds need sugar."

He jumped onto his bike, with a tip of his hat.

Clementine ran to catch up with Giesele. Her face was set, but she linked her arm through Clementine's and they warmed each other as they walked fast through the chill air. They were both pleased to have the biscuits.

There were tattered, ragged clouds in the white sky, heavy with the promise of more snow. Mr. Carter was on the other side of the village green now, greeting a group of GIs. Ernie was with them too, telling them all a joke. The girls saw the soldiers give him a puff on one of their cigarettes.

"Precocious little git," said Clementine.

Giesele laughed.

"Mr. Carter's nice, isn't he?" said Clementine. "I was scared of him at first. I wonder why he's not in the war."

"Maybe flat feet and bad eyes, like Mr. Mildew?"

They giggled.

"My dad has bad eyes too. He feels terrible about not being able to fight. It makes him really angry sometimes." Clementine went on, "Carter doesn't look at all like Mr. Mildew. He's a bit like a film star. Maybe he's an actor like her."

Giesele laughed, "Yes it's a so tragic story – he was a failed actor and became so poor that he had to become a butler. That's why he looks so sad sometimes."

"And that's why he's totally devoted to Frieda and her doomed talent," said Clementine, in a dramatic American accent.

She'd liked what he'd said about their creative minds.

"Shall we ask him to be in the show, too? He can be Clark Gable!" shrieked Clementine.

It was beginning to mizzle thin snow and they started to run towards the village hall – its lights shrouded by black-out material.

Inside the fuggy church hall the Guides were practicing a scene from A Midsummer's Night's Dream. Ethel Wilkins was plodding through Oberon's speech.

"I know a bank where the wild thyme blows
Where oxlips and the nodding violet grow
Quite over-canopied with…"

Even Ethel seemed bored by her own performance. The girls broke off and greeted Clementine and Giesele gratefully.

"We need help! Myrtle says you've got a marvelous plan for the rest of the show," Gertie said.

"The thing is," said Clementine gently, "we need to give the GIs a real treat and remind them of home – I'm not sure how much they'll like Shakespeare,"

"It's totally boring," said Giesele bluntly.

"We need a really good opening." Clementine closed her eyes. Her head was suddenly completely empty. Empty – just a few silly film magazines scattered on a shiny bedspread. Nothing came... until the Marchmont Chest seemed to open in her mind. Its objects flitted and skittered through her head. And the entry from Matilda's diary that she'd read in bed the night before.

"I've got an idea!" she said triumphantly. "We're going to need umbrellas. Lots and lots of umbrellas..."

Chapter 20

Clementine and Giesele were in the sitting room at Cerne House. Frieda was about to perform her song for them. It was twilight and Mr. Carter came in to draw the curtains as the mantel clock struck four. They sat for a moment in the vaporous darkness, until Carter lit the lamps and brought in a tray of tea.

They'd decided that Frieda would appear out of a lightning flash, in a rippling silver satin gown, to sing just before the finale. She was magnificent. The girls watched her, torn and confused. They still had nothing concrete to report to Myrtle - she was a mystery to them and they were both very much under her spell. So everything now hung on what happened on the night of the play – that's when they'd be in Cerne House at eight o'clock – broadcasting time.

Giesele felt a strong connection to home with Frieda and sometimes they lapsed into speaking German. Clementine too felt her as a reminder of stage school and Madame Pearl who was Russian. She talked in her flamboyant and sometimes grand way. Both girls were impressed by her and felt sad for her isolation in this lonely house, in a foreign land.

Clementine became aware of Mr. Carter watching his mistress as she performed and smiling proudly from the doorway as he timed the lighting of the chandelier and practiced lighting the stage flares. He, too, seemed moved by her song.

Frieda smiled at them uncertainly as she finished. Clementine realized she wanted their approval in some way, even though they were just children. She was a huge star and yet she was unconfident. But who was she? Was everything a very clever performance? They started to clap like mad and Frieda nodded.

******

In the church hall the next day, rehearsals for Clementine's big musical number were going slowly. Painfully slowly.

Pam strode over, "We're doing quite well on the umbrella front, Clem. We've collected 16 so far. Some are a bit moth-eaten though."

"Well, keep going," said Clementine. "There's not much time left."

The Guides were eager to learn and had stamina, but their feet had not been trained at Madame Pearl's. School had broken up for Christmas and the show was in a week's time. On Boxing Day hundreds of people would be arriving at Cerne House expecting a proper show for their ticket money.

There were only five days of practice to go.

Clementine sighed. How was she ever going to get twenty-two lumpy girls into perfect flower formation, twirling round, opening their umbrellas in unison, to reveal Myrtle, dressed as Veronica Lake, rising up out of the middle. Myrtle was then going to pull off the lace wedding veil from the Marchmont

Chest, to pose in a flowery sundress. The flowery sundress wasn't yet made, nor had any material been found with which to make it, despite everyone pooling their clothes coupons. Was the whole thing too ambitious? Ugh, it was going to be a disaster!

"This must be how Busby Berkeley feels most of the time," thought Clementine, raking her hands through her hair. She resisted the urge to scratch her head. "And please don't let me have nits, on top of everything else," she prayed silently.

At least the comedy tap dance, with Giesele dressed as Merle Oberon and her as Myrna Loy, was going quite well, though the funny routine, especially their American accents, needed a lot of polishing if the Yanks weren't going to be laughing at them - for the wrong reasons.

Ernie and Ronnie had been practicing with the Disappearing Cabinet: Ronnie was going to magically appear from the "empty cabinet" under the big silk umbrella from the Marchmont chest, and then usher in the Girl Guides in their flower formation.

Ernie and Clinton had been training Orion the dog to perform in the show too. They all loved the clever, sinewy black and white Border Collie now. They couldn't believe he'd so terrified them on their first night. The boys were rather secretive about the act which involved rounding up soldiers from the audience. Ernie had rechristened the dog Oreo, after an American biscuit which he said was black and white and tasted like heaven. But Clementine hadn't been allowed to see any of the act yet and this added to her list of worries.

Clementine's head ached with all the things that could go wrong on the night, in front of hundreds of GIs used to Hollywood silver-screen perfection. The responsibility was exhausting. Sometimes she knew she'd almost lost sight of the reason behind the show. The one Myrtle would say was the real reason: finding out the truth about Frieda Weiss. At just before eight o'clock of course, would come the moment when Frieda would perform her song, sparkling in her silver gown.

Clementine felt quite upset when she thought about it. Silverfish of anxiety flittered through her. She liked Frieda now and Giesele was getting very close to her. They always seemed to be babbling away in German about the theatre in Berlin and liqueur cakes and dress shops and something called Unter den Linden. It made her quite jealous actually. But surely a Nazi spy wouldn't befriend a Jewish girl. And how would she be getting information from the base in the first place? Her head ached really badly now.

Chapter 21

On Christmas Eve, while Ron and Ernie were being forced
to take the first proper bath they'd had since they'd arrived in
Devon, Clementine pulled the big package which had arrived
from home out from under the bed. She'd told the boys to go
and brush their teeth with the "toothpaste" made with ground
cuttlefish Ron had gathered from the beach.

The biggest present, which was for all of them, was a real
Christmas cake, wrapped in greaseproof paper, squeezed into
Gran's biscuit tin. The family must have saved up their entire
sugar rations for weeks. Clementine thought they should present
it to Mrs. Milvaine and Miss Smithers in the morning.

Mum had sent three of dad's big socks for them to hang up for
Santa and there were three wrapped parcels and a card with
handprints from the baby. As Clementine snuffed up a few tears,
she could almost hear Madame Pearl's warning to her girls. "If
you don't blow your nose, the mucus will collect in bags under
your eyes."

The boys hurtled in, unusually clean and scrubbed, in their
pyjamas, to hang up the stockings over the mantelpiece.

"I am never ever, ever going to clean my teeth again. My mouth
tastes like fish guts now." Ernie started breathing his cuttlefish
breath into Clementine's face which soon put a stop to her
homesickness.

Clementine was standing inside a snow globe at the top of a hill. Thousands of uncontrollable umbrellas were prancing around her, laughing hysterically, while she shouted at them, "Come back and line up!" But no sound came out of her sore, dry throat. The umbrellas started whining mockingly at her, "Heesby, Heesby, Heesby, Heesby...."

"He's been…he's been…Clem, wake up! Father Christmas has been…he's been..."

Ronnie was pounding on her chest, desperate to open his stocking. It was five o'clock. The three socks, hanging on the mantelpiece were plumply full. Ronnie bounced delightedly on the bed, squeezing the outside of his stocking and then stuffed his hand in and pulled out a rolled-up copy of The Dandy, some lead soldiers, chestnuts and a carved wooden whistle.

In the boys' parcels were sweaters knitted by Granny Harper, in a rainbow of saved wool, and a stuffed toy owl for Ronnie. He bit into its ear immediately, thrilled.

"He looks very wise," said Clementine.

"He looks like Mr. Churchill!" said Ernie.

"I'm gonna call him Mr. Winston!" squealed Ronnie tucking him under his arm.

Clementine's parcel contained a new pair of satin ballet shoes. Red ones. Where on earth had mum managed to find those in wartime! Her feet were almost too large for them now and as she crammed her toes into the ends, her eyes filled with tears as she thought of mum wrapping them excitedly and all the scrimping she must have done.

She ran to the window to hide her face and balled her hankie fiercely into her eyes. Ernie came up behind her and thrust his present into her hand.

"Happy Christmas, Ginge."

A lipstick: a proper one in a gold, twist-up tube - Revlon's 'Ruby Red'. She'd look like Myrna Loy. Or, better still, Myrtle!

******

Miss Smithers had made corn beef fritters for Christmas breakfast. And Mrs. Milvaine was actually up before nine o'clock! Her face, usually so drawn and sad, looked a bit more alive and she'd dabbed on a sprinkling of face powder. She had a surprise for them. It was a big parcel wrapped in newspaper with holly leaves drawn on it. They unwrapped it to find three flowery costumes for the show, made from the morning-room curtains, for Clementine, Giesele and Myrtle and two black velvet capes for Ernie and Ronnie made from the dining room ones. She'd even made a matching coat for Oreo.

They were all going to the vicarage for Christmas lunch after church. It would be the first time Mrs. Milvaine had left the house and grounds since her son had been declared missing.

She stood gazing uncertainly at her reflection in the hall mirror, until Ernie and Ronnie each grabbed her by an arm and propelled her out of the front door.

Chapter 22

Myrtle had invited Rick, Chuck and some of the other GIs for Christmas lunch and the vicarage was bursting with people.

"Hiya, Red!" Chuck called, when he saw Clementine. He started singing, "She is lost and gone forever...Oh my darlin..." in a tragic voice, like he always did, to tease her but she liked it when he did.

As she was taking napkins into the dining room before lunch, Clementine saw Rick pull Myrtle towards him under the mistletoe, and sweep her up into a kiss. Myrtle laughed and pushed him away, but also seemed quite pleased. Kissing in real life didn't seem to be the same as in films somehow, she thought.

Giesele looked flushed with happiness as she carried past a tray of homemade, toilet roll crackers. "I love Christmas! Everything about it. I never knew how lovely it was."

"Even the sprouts that make you fart?" asked Ernie.

"Yes - even those!" she laughed.

After the turkey there was a huge, flaming Christmas pudding. Ernie found a silver sixpence hidden in his piece and Myrtle found a brass ring and Clementine found a piece of rag, which she nearly swallowed.

"It's a family tradition," explained Mrs. Loame, "Your fortune is in what object you find... the sixpence foretells riches for Ernie, the ring means a marriage for Myrtle and the rag, I'm afraid, means poverty for Clementine. It's just a bit of fun of course."

Myrtle laughed, "Well, I'm definitely not getting married any time soon!"

Clementine was a bit put out. She felt better though when Chuck said, "Great artistes often starve in garrets for a while before they become famous."

"Yeah and really rubbish artistes starve in garrets for ever," snorted Ernie.

******

After lunch they played sardines. Clementine searched all over the house until she found Myrtle, Rick, Chuck, Giesele, Ronnie and Ernie all lying under the big bed in Mr. and Mrs. Loame's bedroom, trying desperately not to giggle. She rolled in underneath to join them on the dusty floor.

They lay there in mild hysteria, shushing each other till Myrtle whispered, "Well, while we're all here, let's just go over the plan for tomorrow night again. Clementine, you'll disappear through the cabinet to go off stage, run up the back staircase and hide in Miss Weiss' bedroom suite, where you will be poised to catch our spy at eight when she will be starting her broadcast."

"If she starts her broadcast…If it's her…" said Clementine.

"Yes… of course - if… Giesele and Ronnie will join you, as soon as they get off stage to help you catch her red-handed, if it is her…"

They all nodded in the dark under the bed.

Myrtle went on, "It's vital that Miss Weiss' song should come dead on five to 8 o'clock – if she rushes off stage to broadcast, we'll catch her in the act. Remember everyone, tomorrow is first and foremost about the mission, not the show. The show's our cover."

Clementine blushed. She was glad they were in the dark and couldn't see her. The show felt very, very important to her and she felt a hot wave of disappointment and irritation. She had been working so hard on it. She almost felt angry with Myrtle.

Chuck spoke in the darkness, "But the guys are all looking forward to the show. It's a huge morale boost for them in these hard times, you know. With them all away from family in the holidays… It's a big deal for them." He squeezed Clementine's shoulder.

Suddenly the light flipped on. Mr. Loame's ruddy face appeared upside down under the bed.

"Aha!" said Mr. Loame - the last one standing.

Everyone shouted, "Sardines!"

Chapter 23

Boxing Day was dull and wet. Clementine's whole body was flickery with anxiety and excitement. Ronnie and Ernie, trapped inside the house, were practicing the disappearing act over and over again in the hall, and it was making her feel quite insane.

At last it was time to go up to Cerne House to make the final preparations for the show. Clinton helped Carter and the Guides set out the chairs that had been gathered from all over the village - wooden ones, floral ones, a gilt dressing table stool, school benches. The odd assortment looked very strange on the shiny floor of the ballroom.

Clementine stood drumming her foot. The dress rehearsal had had to be in the village hall, so goodness knew how it was going to transfer to the very different world of the ballroom. But once the room was lit by the chandelier and candles and Christmas lights, and they'd hung the Guides' strings of gold and silver milk bottle tops, it was starting to look quite magical.

Clementine stood by the stage curtain, which Miss Smithers had made out of old post sacks, checking its hang. Mr. Carter had begged the sacks from Miss Pike and he and Clinton had rigged it up in front of the chandelier. Guides kept filing past her, asking advice about their make-up and props while she tried to tick things off her endless list. She noticed Clinton, in the shadows of the wings, gazing intensely at Giesele who was practicing an arabesque by the side of the stage area.

Clementine was almost shaking with nerves. Everyone seemed to be firing questions or demands at her. Just as she was trying to check through her lighting changes, Mrs. Pumphrey bore down on her and started to talk about the sugar syrup she'd made to serve in the interval – Clementine tried furiously to block out her braying voice.

"I hope you'll serve it while it's warm…I chopped up a mound of sugar beets, boiled them all night to a black pulp then squeezed them in a pillow case under a car jack I borrowed from the postman's van…"

Clementine wanted to scream at her to shut-up.

"Then I boiled the juice again until it formed a black treacle… and the next morning…."

She was so relieved when she saw Mr. Carter approaching to cause a diversion. He'd even brought her a cup of tea.

"That woman is insufferable. Here, have an unbroken biscuit from that other awful Pike woman. Don't worry, my dear. Everything will go swimmingly this evening. Break a leg!"

She could have hugged him. He was even going to do a walk-on appearance, with shoe-polished black hair, as Clark Gable. Clementine finished her tea and launched back in with new energy. Five minutes to go until she would have to change into her own costume. She wished Madame Pearl could see her and everything she'd organised here. She felt a pang. How would she feel about Frieda at eight o'clock? It was all very confusing and worrying and, she had to admit, very exciting.

******

Buttoned tightly into her floral costume, Clementine's palms were sweating as she peeped through the curtains. The audience were taking their seats. Hundreds of GIs and villagers were crowding into the ballroom and pushing along the benches, kitchen chairs and piano stools. There were already so many people that some were standing in the aisles and more would be craning their necks in the hallway.

Mr. Carter had made a huge bowl of hot punch, which was being served as people came in, and they were swigging it back merrily. Nobody seemed very interested in Mrs. Pumphrey's syrup. There didn't seem to be many takers for the Guides' ground acorn 'coffee' either. Giesele appeared behind Clementine and whispered urgently in her ear.

"I don't know what to do. It's Frieda!" She started pulling Clementine by the hand, out of the ballroom.

"Are you mad?", Clementine hissed. "It's curtain-up in five minutes. Ronnie's already getting into the cabinet." She tried to wrench her hand away from Giesele.

"She says she won't go on!"

Clementine ran up the stairs behind her friend. Giesele knocked on the door to Frieda's suite and pushed Clementine inside. The bedroom was like a Ginger Rogers film set and the over-heated scent of orchids made them feel faint. There was a white satin-draped four-poster bed and a vast, walk-in dressing-room lined with mirrors and hat boxes and furs. Sitting at a mother-of-pearl dressing table, her face reflected in a triptych of mirrors, was Frieda. She wore her mask of foundation, but only one eye was made up. It looked huge and tragic and the other looked pink-rimmed and vulnerable, like a little girl's.

Giesele pushed Clementine forward, jabbing her in the spine. She tried to force cheeriness.

"Miss Weiss. It's a full house. Seven minutes till your call. Do you need anything?"

A tiny voice issued from the scarlet mouth.

"I cannot."

"The audience are really excited. They've all come for you, you know," Clementine said.

"I will not. I am sorry."

At once it flashed through Clementine's mind. She doesn't want to go on because she's worried she'll miss making the broadcast. She felt a wave of disappointment and dread. And then Clementine was washed with hot anger.

"You have to. You're a professional. We've worked so hard... the Guides, the boys...everyone's been practising and...collecting things and there are people who have scrimped to buy tickets for their Christmas treat and given their curtains to make costumes and stayed up all night sewing and all for the war effort and to have something to look forward to in this horribly horrible time..." Her anger poured out in torrents, "And now you're acting like a spoilt diva. Do you want them to think you're a Nazi and you don't care about the war! Or can't you do it anymore. Is that why? Remember why you're doing this. It was your idea for it to be a surprise – to show everyone you're a good German."

Giesele gasped. Clementine felt chilled. They held their breath.

It was her red hair again. Why couldn't she control her temper? Clinton was right. Now she'd blown the whole thing. She stepped forward, shaking, to apologise but Frieda stared at her from the mirror and nodded almost imperceptibly. She took up her liquid eye-liner and started painting her naked eye.

Giesele breathed again and they quietly left the room to run back down the stairs.

"Blimey I thought I'd torn it then!"

"Yes, blimey. I also," whispered Giesele.

"Well…Now, we'll know for sure…I sort of don't want to know," said Clementine.

"I too." said Giesele.

"You mean 'me neither'."

"Shut up!"

"Sorry. Well here goes…" Clementine inhaled.

"Thirty seconds till curtain-up," Clementine popped her head into the disappearing cabinet to check on Ronnie, who was crouched inside. His face was scarlet. He was clutching Mr. Winston.

"Clem! I need a wee."

"No you don't. Just hold it."

"I can't!"

"Don't think about fountains or waterfalls. Break a leg, Ronron. You're on."

She signaled to the band to strike up. The band consisted of Pam on her clarinet, Mrs. Loame on the grand piano, Mr. Mildew on the trumpet and Olive on the mouth organ. Mr. Carter winked at her, mouthed "break a leg" and whisked back the curtain to reveal Ernie, in his velvet cloak, posing dramatically in a pool of light.

Ernie's voice squeaked a bit at first, but steadied when the audience gave an encouraging cheer, "And now, for your delectation, a celebration from us English to all our Yank friends. I shall produce for you an evening of marvels..."

He waved his arms over the contraption. There was a flash of orange smoke and the cabinet transformed and collapsed perfectly into the giant silk umbrella, out of which popped Ronnie and Mr. Winston. He leapt up out of the tiny space to huge applause. Clementine saw that Ronnie's legs were painfully clamped together and crossed her fingers that he'd be able to hang on.

Ernie roared, "Look out, it's raining again!" as the twenty-two Girl Guides, under their open umbrellas erupted onto the stage in an almost perfect line of tapping legs and twirling brollies. They whirled together to make a mound of umbrellas and then Myrtle rose up out of their midst in a pool of golden light draped in the demure Victorian wedding veil from the Marchmont Chest. The audience cheered as she pulled off the veil to reveal her sundress and flowery swimming cap.

The increasingly merry crowd of GIs bellowed approval as Myrtle twirled and posed like the movie bathing belle Esther Williams and had a bucket of torn-up-paper 'water' thrown over her by Miss Smithers standing on a ladder by the side of the stage.

The audience clapped and clapped. "Come on! Come on!", thought Clementine anxiously in the wings. They'd run over time if Myrtle took any longer posing and lapping up applause...

At last Myrtle beckoned on Giesele and Clementine who tap danced in smoothly to begin their song and dance routine. Clementine could relax at last now she was actually on stage. Her head felt full of sparkling light and her headache had disappeared. The audience were in great humour. They recognized the famous routine and started singing and clapping along. They roared with appreciative laughter at their Myrna Loy and Merle Oberon skit. More and more of Carter's punch was drunk and the GIs swayed along uproariously on the school benches.

Clementine was lit up with stage-school pride. If only Madame Pearl could see her now. Was Frieda impressed? But then she remembered what they had to do in just a few seconds time.

She and Giesele locked their umbrellas and skipped backwards into the darkness. A flare flashed and then, into the silvery pool of chandelier light, stepped Frieda Weiss. She posed, motionless and the audience became silent, thrilling for a moment to her sphinx-like presence.

It was three minutes to eight o' clock. Three minutes before the broadcast. Just time for Giesele and Clementine to follow Ernie up to Frieda's room. Just time to hide there while she was on stage and to catch her in the act of transmitting when she came off.

In the dark ballroom the audience knew they were in the presence of a real star. As Frieda began to sing 'Lily Marlene,' Giesele and Clementine saw that even Mr. Carter had been moved to tears and had had to slip away from the wings into the shadows. Their hearts thumping, they pulled off their tap shoes and ran up the wide stairs to Frieda's suite. It was nearly 8 o'clock. Frieda was still on stage and she'd only have thirty seconds to get up to her suite and make the coded broadcast. They had to get there before she did and hide. They padded across the darkened room, feet sinking into the thick white carpet. Their torches were hidden in their knickers. They froze.

A tapping was already coming from the dressing room. They crept towards the door. Clementine's heart felt as though it would burst through her ribs. They pushed the door open.

Disorientated for a moment - the dressing room had mirrored doors and walls on all sides - their own faces were reflected back at them in the darting torchlight. Wigs on stands, ballgowns. Mirrored doors slid apart. Beyond the sliding mirrors was a storeroom for furs and cans of film. The tapping grew faster. In a flash of torchlight they took in the metal box of the silent film projector which was hiding a transmitter.

And Carter's face reflected in a dozen mirrors. Carter's hands tapping. His face was sickening. Cold and cruel. It was a mask of hatred under the waxy, stage make-up smile.

"Stupid, interfering Jewish girls!" he spat out in German. Kindly, perfect English-gentleman Mr. Carter, always hanging about joshing with the GIs, befriending Ernie and Ronnie, helping with the show - gossipy and chatty, everyone's friend. He'd been finding out everything there was to know about the village and the military base. The children froze, a sort of seasick horror of betrayal rippling through them.

Carter pulled out a knife and lunged forward, grabbing Giesele round the neck. Clementine screamed and the mirrored door behind Carter swung open onto the back stairs.

Myrtle leapt in behind Carter and knocked the knife from his hand, just as Giesele bit his arm down to the bone. He screamed and swore, shook himself free and ran down the back staircase. The mirrored door had smashed as he slammed away, and shards of mirror cut the girls' stockinged feet as they ran after him. Clementine shouted down to Ronnie and Clinton who were packing up the disappearing cabinet and dressing Oreo in his coat for the finale.

Ernie whistled the dog up. "Oreo quick! Stop Carter!"

The dog snarled at the sweating, hunted man, grabbing at his coat tails, while the children wrestled him into the disappearing cabinet and closed the lid. Ronnie and Giesele sat on top of it to keep him trapped. Oreo stayed on guard, growling and baring his teeth.

Frieda hadn't gone upstairs at all – she'd come straight back on stage to sing an encore. She was singing "Underneath the lamplight by the barrack gate..." and the audience were singing too. "Darling I remember the way you used to wait..." The rapt audience were crying and whooping when Clementine wheeled the cabinet with Ronnie and Giesele sitting on top of it, onto the stage. Frieda was bowing, drinking in the applause, her face was tracked with glittery tears.

Suddenly Myrtle switched on the lights, flooding the ballroom with harsh light.

The sound of furious German swearing was coming from the struggling man in the box. Myrtle announced in a clear voice.

"Ladies and gentlemen. We have discovered a spy...a traitor in our midst."

Frieda froze. The audience weren't sure if this was a comic interlude in the show. But the awkward laughs soon died away. Carter managed to push himself upwards and his shoulders emerged from the cabinet. The Guides immediately sprang into action and surrounded him with their umbrella tips, while Giesele, Clementine and Clinton tied him up with the ropes from the stage curtains.

Myrtle had leapt into the front row and grabbed a gun from one of the amazed lieutenants. She pointed it coolly at Carter by which time Rick and Chuck had made their way onto stage to take over. Myrtle was still in her flowery sundress and swimming cap and a few of the soldiers at the back applauded, still not totally awake to what was happening but the slight air of farcical unreality soon dispersed. This was only too real.

Frieda, horrified, moved towards her servant to confront him. She struck him on the face and walked quietly off stage. He looked broken and shriveled now somehow. At the back of the hall Miss Pike seemed to be having a seizure.

Well, thought Clementine, it had been a grand finale after all.

Chapter 24

Myrtle and Rick helped them piece the story together. Carter's real name was Kurtzheim. Once he'd been taken to the base for interrogation everything was revealed. His father was German and he'd been recruited in Munich because of his perfect English and his experience as an actor. This was to be his finest character role: the perfect English butler, kind and friendly, hating Hitler - he would be assigned by an employment agency to the unknowing film star as she left the country.

He'd been transmitting coded messages each night with information he'd gleaned from Miss Pike and from his friends inside the camp. It had been very easy for him to flatter Miss Pike and pocket any interesting letters from the post office when she was fetching him his tobacco and chocolates. No-one had given away any real information yet about a planned landing in France, but it might easily have happened soon. He'd sent information back and forth in Frieda's film cans too, imprinting the celluloid with a system of dots on the edges of each frame.

Clementine and Giesele talked everything over excitedly as they put the disappearing cabinet, the veil and the tiara carefully back into the Marchmont Chest, rehashing the kaleidoscope of extraordinary events. It hardly seemed real.

"You should put something in from the show…"

"Yes, maybe I shall…I can't imagine I'll ever do anything more exciting than this in my life," said Clementine.

Giesele took her autograph book out of her pocket. There was the page signed by Clementine. "To my dearest, newest and closest friend Giesele." And there was Frieda's flowery message and signature. "To my little stars."

"I wondered perhaps if you might want to....to place this in?" said Giesele.

Cllementine smiled. "You put it in," she said.

It was bitterly cold that afternoon when Giesele and Clementine went into the village shop. Miss Pike was standing at the post office counter. Her face was puffy and liverish, her eyelids swollen, purple. Her eyes flickered over Giesele and then she took something from beneath the counter. It was a stack of letters – at least thirty of them. She held them out to Giesele with trembling hands.

Giesele took the pile of envelopes. They were all addressed to her in the same beautiful, looping handwriting and were postmarked Norfolk. They were dated over seven months. They were all letters from Klara.

"You hid them? You hid my sister's letters? I thought she was dead. She must think that I am," Giesele said, choked.

Miss Pike put her hand up to her thin twitching mouth.

Clementine put her arm round Giesele's shoulders and drew her out of the shop.

******

Clementine lay next to Giesele on her bed in the vicarage as she read the letters feverishly. At last tears rolled down her face and she didn't brush them away. Klara was in Norwich. She'd been moved to another hostel in the countryside and she was teaching young children. She hadn't received any of Giesele's letters, of course, because Miss Pike had kept them all. The letters showed her becoming increasingly frantic with worry and then sure that she'd lost her sister as well as her parents.

Sobs shook Giesele's body and she gave herself up to them. She let Clementine stroke her hair. Klara was safe.

Chapter 25

Miss Pike took to her bed that day and never got up again. Her plump, friendly sister Vi took over the post office.

Clementine and Giesele were in the shop one day after school, buying flour for potato cakes, when Vi told them that two important-looking letters had arrived for them.

Clementine's was from London and she ripped it open straight away. She gasped.

"Mum, the Baby and Gran are going to join us at Mrs. Milvaine's for the rest of the war! Half of the house has been bombed out but Dad insists on carrying on in Camden as an ARP warden. He's gone to bunk in with Uncle Reg in Mornington Crescent."

The other letter was an official one for Giesele. Her hands shook a little as she opened it. She let Clementine read over her shoulder. Myrtle, with the help of Rick and his contacts at The War Office, had managed to arrange to have Klara transferred from Norfolk. She'd be joining Giesele to live at the vicarage. And she'd be teaching the little ones in Ronnie's class at school.

Clementine and Giesele shrieked and jumped up and down amongst the knitting patterns and Oxo cubes, clutching on to each other.

Ernie, who was choosing broken biscuits, scoffed, "Pair of drama queens!" but he was as happy as they were. Vi produced a tin of toffees and a thermos of tea from behind the counter and it became a little celebration in the shop.

******

A flurry of planning letters went back and forth. It was arranged that Klara was going to change trains in London and meet the Harpers at the station. They'd all be arriving in Oxbury together on the afternoon train in a week's time.

It was five minutes to four on a foggy, darkening afternoon. Clementine and Giesele, Ronnie and Ernie were standing on the station platform. They had arrived far too early. Ronnie was running up and down, waving Mr. Winston in the air and doing Winston Churchill impressions which was driving them all mad and making Oreo bark with excitement.

Clinton pulled up by the station gate. He'd brought a cart to carry luggage.

"Blue-eyed Aryan!" Giesele called over. But her eyes were smiling.

Ernie said, "Hey Clem, this'll take your mind off...I'll sing you the new verse of my song for the spring show. How's this?" He started up to the tune of 'My Darling Clementine.'

"Oh my sister, she's a stinker,
oh my stinky Clementine.
She's a ginger and a whinger
Oh that sister of mine..."

But his voice was drowned out for, just at that moment, they heard the sound of the London train steaming towards them. Brakes screeched. Smoke joined fog and doors swung open at the far end of the platform. The children craned their necks to see through the fog as the people climbed down from the train.

An elegant, raven-haired young woman in a navy coat. A plump, red-haired woman, her face wreathed in smiles and tears, holding out her arms wide and a toddler, no longer a baby at all, waddled towards them through the vapourous air.

The children began to run....

Appendix

Kristallnacht – A series of attacks on the Jews by the Nazis on 9th November 1938 throughout Nazi Germany and Austria. The name Kristallnacht comes from the shards of glass that littered the streets after Jewish-owned stores, buildings and synagogues had their windows smashed.

Evacuees - page3 – Children were evacuated from London and other big cities that were considered to be under threat of being bombed by the Germans. They were sent to the countryside to live with host families.

Blackout - page 5 – During the war people had to cover their windows to prevent any glimmer of light being visible from the outside so as to not risk aiding the enemy in their bombing raids.

Blitz - page 20 – The Blitz occurred between September 1940 and May 1941. It was an intense bombing of London and other major cities in the UK by the Germans. Two million houses were destroyed and 32,000 civilians killed and 87,000 injured. (http://www.primaryhomeworkhelp.co.uk/war/blitz.htm)

Kindertransport - page 30 - Camp in East Anglia – Jewish children were transported to England from Germany, Poland, Czechoslovakia and Austria before the start of World War II. They were held temporarily in a camp in East Anglia while they were placed with foster families.

Bomb shelters in the Underground - page 37 – People sheltered deep underground in the London Underground during World War II with an estimated 170,000 people finding shelter there during the bombing raids in the war.

Spam - page 41 - Originated in the USA and arrived in Britain in 1941. Because of lack of access to fresh meat during the war Spam became a very popular item. *(www.spam-uk.com)*

Gas Masks - page 42 - People were given gas masks to protect themselves from a possible gas attack from the Germans, though in fact a gas attack was never carried out on the British during the war.

Powdered Egg - page 52 - Was introduced in 1942 in a response to fresh eggs being rationed. A tin would contain the equivalent of a dozen eggs and was on top of your fresh egg ration which meant people could use them to make cakes or scrambled eggs. *(http://www.historylearningsite.co.uk/dried_eggs.htm)*

Girl Guides collecting tin foil - page 58 - The Girl Guides helped a lot with the war effort and one of the things they did was collect tin foil. The foil was used to make bullets and shells. It was also shredded and then dropped from aircraft as they entered enemy airspace to confuse radar-controlled weapons. *(http://ggwa100years.com/2014/10/20/snippets-of-history-girlguides- wa-in-world-war-ii/)*

Acorn coffee - page 114 - In World War II, lots of foods were rationed and coffee was quite hard to come by so acorns were often used to make a coffee-substitue, as were roasted chicory and grain.

Elements of the story are loosely based on the plans for the D-Day landings rehearsed at the US base in Tiger Bay in Devon.

Lyrics from 'My Darling Clementine'

"My Darling Clementine" - The words to the American comic, ironically-tragic song which is sung and quoted by various characters in the book *(www.metrolyrics.com)*:

Near a cavern, across from a canyon,
Excavating for a mine,
Lived a miner, forty-niner
And his daughter Clementine

Oh my Darling, Oh my Darling,
Oh my Darling Clementine.
You are lost and gone forever,
Dreadful sorry, Clementine.

Light she was and like a fairy,
And her shoes were number nine
Herring boxes without topses
Sandals were for Clementine.

CHORUS:

Drove she ducklings to the water
Every morning just at nine,
Hit her foot against a splinter
Fell into the foaming brine.

CHORUS:

Ruby lips above the water,
Blowing bubbles soft and fine,
But alas, I was no swimmer,
So I lost my Clementine.

CHORUS:

How I missed her! How I missed her!
How I missed my Clementine,
Till I kissed her little sister,
And forgot my Clementine.

CHORUS:

Then the miner, forty-niner,
Soon began to peak and pine,
Thought he oughter join his
daughter,
Now he's with his Clementine.

CHORUS:

In the church yard in the canyon
Where the myrtle doth entwine
There grows roses and other posies
Fertilized by Clementine.

Thanks

Thanks to Frances Cain, big boss lady and mastermind behind A Girl for All Time®, for her commitment to publishing intelligent stories for girls and making beautiful dolls. To Rebecca Wolff who edited the book. To Peter Salmi for his starry doodle drawings and invaluable plot advice and to my son Raphael for reading a first draft and warning me where things were "getting boring or sickly".

I found 'The Children's War' by Juliet Gardner, the companion catalogue to the excellent Imperial War Museum exhibition, wonderfully useful when researching Clementine's Winter,

A special thank you to Louise Robinson for her inspiring cover artwork and her illustrations of Giesele and of Clementine Skating.

A Girl For All Time®

Explore the world of A Girl for All Time®, a series of award-winning British historical dolls, novels and keepsake books that bring the past to life with exquisite fashions, exciting stories and original activities to share with friends and family.

Matilda, Your Tudor Girl,™ has decreed that her travelling chest and its treasures shall be passed down to the first born girl in each generation of the Marchmont family, to inherit on her thirteenth birthday.

And so we follow the first born girls of the Marchmont family through 500 years of intrigue and adventure.

Each character tells her own thrilling story through accompanying novels and beautiful costumes, which are brought to life in customizable Keepsake Books, yours to keep and treasure forever.

This uniquely British brand encourages intelligent, creative play for girls 6 and older, specializing in gorgeously crafted 16" vinyl dolls, historically inspired novels and activity books, costumes and more.

Immerse yourself in the world of A Girl For All Time®, the perfect gift for that someone special.

Available now at www.AGirlForAllTime.com

Matilda, Your Tudor Girl™
Lydia, Your Georgian Girl™
Amelia, Your Victorian Girl™
Clementine, Your 1940s Girl™

Matilda's Secret
Norfolk, 1540
"Nothing exciting will ever happen to me"

Thirteen-year old Matilda Marchmont lives a dull life in the
country – riding her horse, mixing her family's medicines,
imagining herself to be a witch and writing in her secret diary.
She longs for the glamour and thrills of life at court, led by
her ultra-fashionable young cousin Katherine Howard.
And then one night something DOES happen. She is to be
sent to court too, as lady-in-waiting and spy, to help further
Katherine's marriage chances with King Henry VIII himself.
Matilda is drawn into a glittering world of intrigue, intense
friendship and mortal danger which takes her from Hampton
Court Palace to the Bloody Tower itself.

Matilda's Keepsakes and Secrets Book
Your own customisable keepsake book

Plan a Tudor themed sleep over with your friends, make delicious Tudor treats, try Tudor vibed hair and fashion ideas, or make your own family tree.

Re-imagine Matilda's world for yourself and your friends and make a keepsake book you will treasure forever.

Amelia's Inheritance
London, 1880

Amelia Elliot was half way down the stairs to the school dining hall when her life changed forever.

Before the gong sounded for tea she was an ordinary schoolgirl looking forward to her thirteenth birthday and worrying about her Latin exam. After the gong, she was an orphan sent hurtling into a shadowy world of subterfuge, treachery and unlikely friendship.

In a fight to reclaim the mysterious family chest left to her by her Tudor ancestor Matilda, Amelia begins a thrilling journey which will lead her from glittering ballrooms to the slums of the rookeries, from society seances to the lime-lit stages of the London music hall.

Lydia in the New World
Boston, 1780

Lydia Peyton had got used to the idea of never seeing
home again. England and Bristol, were they still even home?

She supposed Boston was home now. But even now that her legs
had stopped rolling with the memory of being on board ship for
weeks and weeks, here she was in the New World and still feeling
strange. No friends and nothing familiar - even the star-shaped
flowers in the pretty garden were strange.

There was the intriguing girl she'd seen in town this morning
outside the haberdashery store. A girl with caramel-coloured skin
and raven hair in two long bound plaits and a dress of glossy
leather. She was with her father who was delivering a pile of fur
pieces to the back of the shop. Could she become a friend ?

The girl looked friendly and mischieveous... Maybe Lydia would
go back tomorrow for some more silk roses for her hat and see if
the girl were there again...

Lydia in the New World will be published in 2016.

Note on the author

Sandra Goldbacher is a screenwriter and director.

She is known for her twice BAFTA nominated feature films:
The Governess, starring Minnie Driver, set in the 1850s;
Me Without You starring Michelle Williams, and Ballet Shoes
a BBC Christmas adaptation of the children's classic by Noel
Streatfeild, starring Emma Watson. She directed the opening
episodes of Golden Globe-winning The Hour 2, a BBC2 drama
set in 1950s London, starring Dominic West.

Sandra wrote MATILDA's SECRET, the first in the series of
A Girl for all Time® novels and the next in the series,
AMELIA's INHERITANCE, set in Victorian London.
Sandra is endlessly drawn to stories about the complicated
interactions of young women. Sandra lives in London with
her husband and son.

Awards

Oppenheim Toyportfolio
4 time Platinum Winner

Dolls Magazine
Winner: Industry Choice Award 2013
Nominee 'Playdoll of the Year 2013"
Winner: Industry Choice Award 2014
Winner 'Playdoll of the Year 2014"

Toy Talk
Best Doll 2011
Best Doll 2012
Best Doll 2013

Good Toy Guide
Seal of Approval 2011
Seal of Approval 2012
Seal of Approval 2013

Toy Shop UK
Commended 2012

MUMSChoice
TOP 5 GIRLS TOY

Mum's Choice
Top Five Girls Toys